SING SOFTLY
TO ME

**Center Point
Large Print**

**This Large Print Book carries the
Seal of Approval of N.A.V.H.**

SING SOFTLY TO ME

Dorothy Garlock

CENTER POINT PUBLISHING
THORNDIKE, MAINE

This Center Point Large Print edition
is published in the year 2008 by arrangement with
Grand Central Publishing,
a division of Hachette Book Group USA.

The text of this Large Print edition is unabridged.
In other aspects, this book may vary
from the original edition.
Printed in the United States of America.
Set in 16-point Times New Roman type.

ISBN: 978-1-60285-341-6

Library of Congress Cataloging-in-Publication Data

Garlock, Dorothy.
  Sing softly to me / Dorothy Garlock. -- Center Point large print ed.
    p. cm.
  ISBN 978-1-60285-341-6 (lib. bdg : alk. paper)
  1. Large type books. I. Title.

PS3557.A71645S55 2008
  813'.54--dc22

2008032897

For my lifelong friend
Marie Hook
Oklahoma City, Oklahoma

CHAPTER ONE

"Burr . . . I must have holes in my head to live here!"

The muttered words came from lips stiff with cold. Snow covered the trees, bushes, and sidewalks, reflecting the feelings of the young woman who hurried toward the large, brick building that loomed ahead of her. A feeling of coldness permeated her, spreading its numbness to her fingers and toes.

"Oops!" Her foot hit an icy spot. She regained her balance and pulled her striped stocking cap farther down over her ears. "I'll be late *again,"* she moaned. Five A.M.! she thought. What an ungodly hour!

The cars that passed beneath the streetlights were eerie, shrouded in fog, as were the forms that hurried toward the building, their breath suspended in the cold northern air.

Passing through the entrance of St. John's Hospital, Beth nodded to several acquaintances who were coming off duty and heading home to warmth and companionship. Their exclamations at the raw bitterness of the winter weather were soon lost to her. She walked briskly down the highly polished corridor to the nurses' lounge, where she shed her coat and hung it in her locker. She adjusted the starched white cap on her thick, dark hair and ran down the hall to the elevator.

The sixth-floor bell sounded as the elevator slid to a silent halt. The doors opened to a busy scene of nurses, doctors, orderlies, and other medical personnel.

"Oh, damn!" Beth murmured nervously as she hurried to the nurses' station. Her eyes were intent on the stiff back of her supervisor, who stood checking a chart with a young nurse. She was late again!

"Did he find you?" A clear voice came from beyond the still backs and bent heads.

Beth turned to find her friend Jill smiling at her. "Find who?" she asked.

"You. A man was just here looking for you. I told him you came on duty about ten minutes ago and probably went up to check on young Joshua in room six thirty-five. He went in that direction. You've obviously missed him." Jill came from behind the desk. "You'd remember him if—" She broke off suddenly, flipped open the metal chartboard in her hand, and began to explain the doctor's instructions for a new patient.

"And what is your excuse this morning, nurse?" An authoritative voice came from behind.

Before Beth could conjure up an answer, the Dragon, as the supervisor was called by the staff, was paged over the intercom. Both nurses sighed with relief when the elevator doors closed behind her.

"It only postpones my chewing out." Beth sighed.

"Yeah. She won't forget. But I want to tell you about this guy who's looking for you. He's tall . . . rugged, and all man! He looks just like the cowboy

8

in the cigarette ads, I swear he does. I can just see him riding the range, roping a cow, doggin' a steer, or whatever they do. Oh, glory! There he is!"

Beth felt her cheeks grow warm. Her eyes encountered lively gray-green eyes. She could feel him appraising her from the top of her nurse's cap to the tips of her white shoes. He continued his inspection while his long strides covered the diminishing space between them. His large, muscular frame was covered by a shearling coat, unbuttoned, and a rich, bottle-green sweater. A brown Stetson was pulled low over his wide forehead and rested above straight dark brows—dark as the thick, bushy mustache that accented his strong, frowning mouth. His intense gaze held hers, making her aware of his sheer, powerful masculinity in a way that sent a shiver of panic through her.

"I've looked all over this damn hospital for you, Beth." His voice was deep, husky, and held more than a hint of annoyance.

Beth's blue eyes remained fixed on him. "I just came on duty,"

"I need coffee. Where's the cafeteria?" He moved to take her arm, but she stepped back.

"Follow the sign, you can't miss it," she said carefully, staring up at his stern face. "I'm on duty. I can't leave the floor."

"When do you get a break?"

"About nine. But I don't always take one."

"And you won't this morning."

"No."

"I'm neither rapist nor mugger, Elizabeth."

"What do you want, Thomas? Why are you here? Has something happened to Sarah? Has she had an . . . accident?" Her head began to spin. That's why he's here! My sister had an accident!

"No, she hasn't. I'm sorry if I scared you. I've been driving all night and I'm tired and hungry. I need to talk to you." His voice grew louder with his impatience.

"That's a relief, but lower your voice." Beth glanced at Jill, who stood gaping at him with a dreamy look on her face. Beth had to admit he was something to gape at, but Jill, who stood frozen in admiration, was making a fool of herself.

Beth's gaze came back to Thomas Clary. He hadn't changed one bit during the last three years. He was still as confident, still as arrogant, still as overpowering as he had been when he came to attend the wedding of her sister and his brother. She had been nineteen then, and helpless with adoration. Now she was twenty-two, and far more capable of assessing a man.

"How've you been, Beth?"

"Fine." She didn't look at him. What the hell did he care? He'd gone away without a word. He'd kissed her, squired her around her hometown for a week— had made her fall in love with him. She'd waited, thinking he'd call. It had taken a year for her to get over him. Now here he was . . . in living color!

His eyes assessed her critically, moving over her short, shiny brown hair, to the big blue eyes with their dark lashes. His eyes narrowed as he gazed at her mouth, and her lips trembled at the image that came swiftly to mind—Thomas taking possession of her mouth, kissing her as she had never been kissed, making the kisses she shared later with other men seem almost . . . boring. His gaze traveled to the firm breasts rounding out the white uniform, and he smiled a secret smile while she burned with resentment. Slowly, coolly, he let his eyes roam over her from the narrow waist, down over slim hips and long legs to the tips of her white shoes, and back to her eyes, now sparking with indignation.

"You're thinner, and . . . more beautiful."

She did her best to return his gaze coolly. What she really wanted was to tell him to get the hell out and never come back. Instead, she said, "You'll have to excuse me. I've got my rounds to make."

His brows came together in a scowl of displeasure, and a pleased flutter punctuated her already rapid heartbeat.

"Just a minute." His massive body shifted to block her path. "I've driven nine hundred miles in the last two days and I'm dead tired. I'll go take a nap and be at your place at six o'clock. You be there." He turned abruptly on his heel and walked away.

"Wow! You've been holding out on me," Jill accused, after he was gone.

Beth was in a perplexed state of shock. Thomas

Clary, here. Three years ago she would have given anything to see him come striding down the corridor toward her. But now she wanted no attachments. He'd broken her heart once. It had been like the end of the world for her, as if she had walked off a cliff or into an airplane propeller. She had almost failed to pass her exams because of him. She had wanted to scream, tear her hair out, or lie down and die. She had done none of those things. She did the only thing possible for her to do—put him out of her mind and wrapped herself in her work.

Now she wished desperately that he hadn't come. He had said Sarah was all right. "So what does he want with me?" she wondered, her thoughts swirling in confusion. She tried without success to force the image of his dark face and green eyes from her mind.

Jill was still babbling about the "cowboy," and Beth was lost in thought when the Dragon reappeared, causing both women to flee to their respective duties.

The busy activities of the day helped Beth keep the evening confrontation with Thomas from her mind. Three babies were born during her shift, one premature. The infant needed the expert care that Beth was qualified to give, so her day was spent in the busy routine of helping to save, then monitor the tiny bundle of life which the parents had so eagerly awaited.

When the shifts changed, Beth stayed on to discuss the needs of the fragile premie with the oncoming nurse. By the time she headed home, she was drained and longed for a good soak in a hot tub.

The weather had worsened during the day. Blowing snow was whirling through the streets, stalling traffic, and Beth was thankful her small apartment was only a few blocks away. She hurried along, even jaywalking in her haste to get to her apartment. Home, she thought. It's not much, but it's mine. One large cozy room with a tiny kitchen, a small bedroom, and a minute bath was the place she called home.

Beth reached the large old Victorian house, and in her haste to get in out of the cold she almost collided with her neighbor Mrs. Maxwell on the porch.

"I'm sorry. I didn't see you," she exclaimed, steadying the elderly lady.

"I'm all right, dear. I just stepped out to check the weather and get the paper." The tiny woman smiled up at Beth.

"Be careful. The porch is slippery. You don't want a broken leg."

"I should say not. It would cut down on my dancing."

"You're incredible!" Beth smiled.

"You're only as old as you think you are, my dear. And while you're still young, you'd better get you a man before all the good ones are taken."

"Trying to get rid of me, huh?"

"You'd have a lot more fun," Mrs. Maxwell confided with a giggle.

Beth laughed and stomped the snow from her shoes. Inside she climbed the curved staircase to the second floor and unlocked her door. Two apartments shared the floor and hers was the smaller one, but it had a small fireplace in the living room, and she loved the high ceilings and long windows. She had often reflected on what an elegant home it must have been in the early years, before it was converted into apartments.

Keeping her thoughts carefully away from the coming meeting with Thomas, she put the teakettle on to boil, turned on the stereo and listened to the classical strains of a concerto. She made a cup of tea and carried it with her to the bathroom.

Ten minutes later she was relaxing in a steamy, hot bath. Just what I need to loosen the kinks in my back and neck, she mused, and sank deeper in the claw-footed tub, until the water reached her chin. With her eyes closed, she allowed her mind to dwell on the early morning meeting that had shaken her to the core.

Thomas had come all the way from Wyoming to see her. What could he possibly want to talk to her about? It was urgent, she realized, otherwise he wouldn't have come directly to the hospital after driving all night. It had to be something to do with Sarah.

Beth and her sister had not been close while growing up. That was due partly to the thirteen-year difference in their ages and partly to the fact that they were half-sisters. Sarah was ten years old when her mother died. It had been a horrendous blow to the sensitive young girl. Her father had tried to bridge the gap, but Sarah's adolescence and hurt all contrived to push him further from her. She returned to her boarding school after the funeral, a grieving, unhappy little girl. Two years later her father remarried and Beth was the result of that marriage. Sarah's stepmother tried with love and understanding to break through the tough barrier that surrounded the young girl, and eventually she succeeded. By the time Sarah was ready to go out on her own, she and her stepmother had developed a warm, loving relationship.

After Sarah was graduated from college, she took a teaching job at an American military base in Europe, then transferred to other bases around the world. She met Steven Clary, an American service man, and when he was discharged they came to Minnesota to be married. At that time Beth was nineteen, in her second year of nurse's training, and ripe to fall desperately in love with the man who came out from Wyoming to be his brother's best man.

A year later both her parents died in a freak accident caused by a faulty furnace. Beth sent a telegram to Sarah, who came immediately. They made funeral arrangements, grieved together, and took comfort in knowing that they were sisters and had each other.

Beth was jarred from her thoughts by a loud

knocking on her door. Mrs. Maxwell, she muttered silently. You're a darling, but sometimes a pest. She got out of the tub, wrapped a huge towel around her, and went to the door, fully expecting to have a bowl of chicken soup or something equally nourishing thrust into her hands.

"Interesting." Tom's gray-green eyes traveled from her startled face down to her wet, bare shoulders, then down to her breasts, barely concealed by the clinging towel. "May I come in?" he asked, then walked into the room, leaving her holding the door.

"It's only five o'clock! I didn't expect you so soon," Beth protested.

"No? I'd have sworn you did." Amusement played over his face as his eyes toured her figure. Beth's cheeks flamed.

"Make yourself at home," she invited sarcastically as he removed his coat. With as much dignity as possible, she stalked across the room.

"I'll be glad to help—"

She slammed the door on his words, and fumed. Damn him for coming early! She quickly toweled herself dry and pulled a pair of snug jeans up over her long slim legs. She was annoyed with herself for not thinking that he might show up before the appointed time. After slipping on a light blue turtleneck and a bulky navy sweater, she ran a brush through her hair. She was glad for once that it curled on its own. Looking at her reflection in the mirror, she applied a touch of lipstick.

The young woman who looked back at her had short, dark hair cut in a wedge that showed the tips of her ears then tapered to the nape of her neck. She had deep blue eyes set far apart and fringed with dark lashes; a small, straight nose that even in the middle of winter was covered with freckles; high cheekbones, her best feature, she thought; and a soft, luscious mouth that she thought was too wide. I'm as common looking as an old shoe, she thought as she looked at herself. Oh, what I'd give for a little more sophistication.

Tom was sprawled on the couch. His eyes swept over her and he grinned. "I prefer the towel."

Beth, usually ready with a comeback, could think of nothing to say. She felt a telltale warmth invade her cheeks again. Damn him!

"What do you want to talk about?" she asked crossly.

"I'll tell you over dinner." He got to his feet, slung on his coat, then plucked hers from the rack beside the door.

She folded her arms across her breasts and waited, her eyes looking unflinchingly into his. "Is this your way of inviting me to dinner?"

"Should I have sent an engraved invitation?" He grinned cockily.

"Did it ever occur to you that I may already have a dinner date?" Her chin lifted and there was rebellion in every line of her body. He gazed at her defiant face with such intensity that she almost cringed. He knows! she thought. He knows that I was desperately in love with him!

"No. Now stop hedging and c'mon. You know you're going, I know you're going, so let's go."

"You haven't changed a bit," she flared. "You're still as conceited as ever." Her voice lashed him with bitter, unguarded words.

"Yeah?" His smile said he was proud of it. "You've changed. You didn't use to be so shrewish. I remembered you as being a real sweet little girl."

There was amusement in his voice. She wanted to retort that she was no longer the young, gullible, *little girl* she'd been three years ago. It had taken her a long time to erase his image from her subconscious. Night after night she had dreamed of him, despising herself for her inability to control her mind. But she had conquered her obsession for him, and now here he was, bulldozing his way back into her life. She wanted to put up further resistance, but what was the use? Clinging tightly to her dignity, she slipped her arms into the sleeves of the down coat he was holding for her.

"Button up. It's freezing out there."

Beth pulled the hood of her parka up over her head and put on her mittens. Then, holding fast to her resentment, she stalked ahead of him out the door.

It was dark outside now, and the temperature had dropped. An icy gust of air met them at the door. Tom took her arm and propelled her toward a four-wheel drive vehicle parked across the street. Once inside he quickly started the engine and turned on the heat.

"It'll take a minute to warm up. God! It's cold here," he grumbled.

Beth huddled far down inside her coat, wishing fervently that she had one as warm as his. She was shivering, almost uncontrollably, from nerves and the cold. It was impossible to keep her teeth from chattering.

"You sound like a typewriter." He laughed and gave her a sideways glance.

"It's not funny, dammit!"

"You'll be warm in a minute."

This is crazy, she thought. Why did I come out with him? What in the world does he want to talk about? He could have said what he had to say in my nice warm apartment. They drove in silence, while Beth's mind churned with curiosity.

"I understand the Depot is a good place to eat." His statement broke the silence and hung in the cold air between them.

"I wouldn't know. I never eat there." The Depot was the classiest restaurant in town. That kind of dining wasn't covered in her budget. She was sure of one thing—she wasn't dressed for a place like that. Her mind was still working feverishly as they parked in front of the old building that housed the finest eating establishment Rochester, Minnesota, had to offer.

"I'm not sure about this." Her blue eyes sought his.

"Why?"

19

"I'm not dressed for this place."

The firm lips twitched under the dark mustache. "Don't worry. You look fine. You just might be the best-looking woman here if you took that frown off your face."

He laughed at the look of exasperation that followed the frown, and got out of the car. With great reluctance she opened the door and stepped out onto the snowpacked drive. The wind buffeted her as she walked beside the tall man who held her arm in a powerful grip. They passed through the double doors of the restaurant and into the warmth of the elegant interior.

They were met by a hostess dressed in a long velvet skirt and silk blouse. She glanced briefly at Beth as Tom helped her out of her parka, then dismissed her and gave her attention to him. Beth felt terribly conspicuous in her jeans and sweater, but managed to appear nonchalant as she followed the hostess, very conscious of Tom close behind her. They were ushered to a quiet table, partially secluded from the view of the other diners.

One glance at the menu told Beth she was definitely out of her league. There were no prices on the menu! Fighting not to let herself be intimidated by this place or this man, she armed herself with her pride. She glanced at the menu, and gave Tom her preferences with cold formality.

Once their order was taken by the waiter, who seemed to materialize as if by magic, Tom settled back in his chair, indifferent to his surroundings. His eyes settled on Beth. She looked everywhere but at him, causing a slight smile to twitch at his lips.

"You're going to have to look at me sometime, you know."

"Thomas—"

"Sarah, my mother, and you are the only people who have ever called me Thomas."

His softly spoken words caught her by surprise, causing her to look straight into his eyes. Once captured, she couldn't look away. He continued to study her, his eyes traveling over her flushed cheeks, flashing blue eyes, and the tip of her tongue, which darted out to moisten her suddenly dry lips.

Beth despised herself for blushing. It was a curse that at her age color could flood her face at the most inopportune times. She forced herself to return the stare in exactly the same way he was eyeing her. He was a handsome man—rugged and very masculine. He's a man's man, she thought. A man another man could depend on. He's a woman's man too.

Deciding that the best defense was a good offense, she attacked. "Okay. You've played your little game long enough. You've got me dangling in suspense—so out with it."

"I want you to come back to Wyoming with me."

It took several seconds for Beth to grasp what he'd said. "Go . . . with you to Wyoming? You can't be serious."

"Oh, but I am." He wasn't smiling.

"But . . . but—"

He raised his hand to silence her as the waiter approached with their dinner. He watched the expressions flitting across her face, and it occurred to him that, although she wasn't what would be considered a beautiful woman, she certainly was the most *alive* woman he'd met in a long while. Where was the naive child he'd known three years ago? After the wedding he'd kicked himself all the way back to Wyoming for staying a week instead of the three days he'd planned. They had danced, swam, gone to the races, laughed at each other's bad jokes. To him, it had been a pleasant interlude. He'd not realized until the very last day that Sarah's little sister might have a crush on him.

"First we're going to eat our dinner," he said when they were alone again. "Mainly because I'm starved, and also because you'll be more rational with a full stomach."

"You've lost a few bricks!" The words were dumb, juvenile, and she was instantly ashamed of them. But dammit, his presence was disturbing. She thought that, at the age of twenty-two she had a reasonable amount of poise and confidence. She had worked for a year in the emergency room at the hospital and had seen the ugly side of life—atrocities she'd not even imagined. She'd been proud of the way she handled herself, but her self-confidence was nothing compared to what *he* carried around.

The meal was delicious—cooked to perfection

and served beautifully. Beth ate, but hardly tasted what she was eating. Her mind and her stomach were not at all compatible. Go to Wyoming? What for? Sarah was all right—he'd said so. She waited for him to finish eating, furious that he could eat such a large meal as if nothing momentous had happened. He finally finished and the after-dinner wine was poured. She could contain her curiosity no longer.

"Will you *please* say what you've come to say," she demanded.

"As I told you before, I want to take you back home with me."

"I'm not deaf! You said that thirty minutes ago. Why?"

The large masculine hand lifted the fragile wine glass, swirling its contents before lifting it to smiling lips. "Because I want you to."

A flash of anger engulfed her. He's playing with me and enjoying every minute of it! She ground her teeth in mute rage, grabbed her bag and got to her feet.

Tom reached out and grasped her wrist. "I'm sorry, Beth. Sit down. Somehow, I can't resist teasing you. You rise to the bait so beautifully."

She resumed her seat but remained poised for flight. He took his hand from her arm, but the warmth of his touch remained, sending danger signals up to her flustered brain, telling her that if she made one move, his hand would snake out again faster than a whiplash. "Sarah has multiple sclerosis."

"Oh! Oh, my God! Why didn't you tell me at—"

"Don't worry. They think the disease has been arrested."

"Arrested? Arrested?" she blurted angrily. "For how long?"

He ignored her outburst and spoke calmly. "Sarah's been staying with me ever since she found out about the illness. Up until now she's been able to manage on her own, with the help of my housekeeper. But she needs someone with knowledge of the disease. She needs her sister, the nurse."

"Why didn't she tell me?"

"She didn't want to upset your life."

"But she's my sister!" She looked away from him, her face pale.

"Yes."

Beth's medically-trained mind clicked into gear. "How long has she known?"

"A year."

"A year? Then it must have been discovered right after Steven was killed."

"It was. She didn't let me get in touch with you then, because you were about to take your Minnesota board, and she thought it was more important for you to get your nursing license than to come to Wyoming to be with her."

Beth groaned, remembering. Sarah had called her shortly after Steven's accident to tell her when the funeral would be. Beth hadn't especially liked her sister's husband, but she'd wanted to go out to be with Sarah. But Sarah had refused, saying she was fine, there were lots of friends who were helping out. And she'd insisted it was more important for Beth to get her nursing license. She'd said very little about Steven's accident—she seemed reluctant to talk about it, and Beth had never pressed her for details— and never mentioned her illness.

"Why didn't you bring her here to the Mayo Clinic?" Beth demanded, needing to lash out at someone, wanting an excuse to be angry.

"I tried, but she wouldn't come. She's had the best medical care available. What she needs now is companionship, someone close to her."

"She's had you. Or are you too busy to give her your time?" She knew she was being unreasonable. She could tell by the look in his eyes that he thought so too. But his eyes also told her that he understood the hurt that was making her irrational.

"She doesn't know I've come for you. I'm sure she wouldn't want to interfere with your life."

"It'll take me a while to make arrangements to leave."

"I'm starting back the day after tomorrow. That's enough time."

"I can't leave that soon. I'll have to give notice at the hospital. I can't just pull out and leave on a moment's notice. I'll come out in a few weeks."

The waiter came with the bill. Tom paid him, and the waiter acknowledged the generous tip.

The cold air, when they left the restaurant, revived Beth's senses somewhat. She was still in a numbed state over the news of Sarah's illness. The drive back to her apartment seemed to take only seconds, and they didn't speak until he parked the Blazer in front of the old Victorian house. Leaving the motor running, he switched off the lights and turned to her. Despite her inner turmoil, she was terribly conscious of him. To her extreme discomfort, he sat studying her. The light from the streetlight shone on his face, and when she looked at him, his eyes held hers relentlessly.

"This afternoon I took the liberty of speaking to your supervisor. She agreed to give you a leave of absence due to the family emergency. . . ." He paused while she drew an angry breath. "Starting tomorrow."

"You had no right to do that! I can take care of my own business, thank you! I'm not a child."

He gave a low whistle. "No, siree. You certainly are not a child, *now.*"

She could see the flash of white teeth, and knew he was laughing at her. Her Irish temper flashed out of control.

"You're arrogant and hateful and . . . belong in the looney bin!" Too furious to go on, she opened the door to escape his hateful presence.

His low laugh only increased her anger. "You're just a bundle of cheer. I can see that we'll have a great time on the way home."

"Forget the *we* stuff, mister! When you leave, it will be without me!" She slammed the door with all her might, and ran up the walk to the safety of her home.

CHAPTER TWO

There was a great deal on Beth's mind as she got ready to leave for her sister's home. Sarah's condition was always in her thoughts—how could she not worry about her, especially when she hadn't seen her in such a long time? Beth wished she'd been there to help her sister with all she'd been going through—Steven's death and her illness.

There were also her apartment, friends, and most important, her job being left behind. Her call to her supervisor had confirmed that she'd been given a leave of absence.

"It's perfectly understandable," the Dragonlady had said, as if butter wouldn't melt in her mouth. "Mr. Clary told me of the difficulty in finding a live-in nurse and insisted that I call your sister's doctor. The doctor spoke highly of Mr. Clary and said he was one of Cody's leading citizens. Mr. Clary explained why it was so necessary for you to leave at once."

He explained, Beth thought with irritation. I'll just bet he did, and oozed charm while he was doing it.

Resentment and frustration over Tom's high-handed method of ending her employment increased until her anger overflowed when he knocked on her apartment door two mornings later. She considered, for several wild moments, refusing to open it. She could easily ship her things and catch a plane for Wyoming.

"Eliz-a-beth! Do you want me to kick up a hell of a racket out here?" he shouted after the tenth rap on the door.

She flung open the door. He stalked in and picked up her suitcases without comment, seeming oblivious to her anger.

They left Rochester in the eerie morning darkness, headed south, then west on the interstate. Beth sank down in her seat and buried her face in the fur collar of her parka. Exhaustion overcame her, and with an odd sense of detachment, she promptly fell asleep. She woke once, conscious of the motion of the truck, then it lulled her back into an uneasy sleep, her head resting uncomfortably against the door.

Sometime later the sudden stillness of the truck awakened her. The only sound she heard was the soft purring of the motor.

"Wake up, sleeping beauty. We're making a pit stop."

"Where are we?"

"We're on Interstate 90. I need to stretch my legs and use the facilities."

Beth sat up, stretching her cramped body, trying to ease the kinks in her back. A wide yawn escaped her, but she quickly covered her mouth with the back of her hand.

"You've got the classiest snore I ever heard."

"I don't snore!" she snapped. She knew he was teasing her, but she welcomed the excuse to vent her anger at him.

He smiled, clearly amused. "C'mon. The nippy air'll perk you up."

She didn't want to leave the warmth of the truck, but reluctantly followed him up the path to the brick building operated by the Minnesota Highway Department.

Later, through a dull headache, she watched Tom come out of the building and down the walk toward her. Even in her anger she had to admit that he was something to look at. The shearling coat and Stetson added to his charisma. Jill's comparison of him to the man in the cigarette ads was accurate. Tom Selleck, move over, here comes Tom Clary! she thought.

"Feel better now?" he asked, as he threw his coat into the backseat before getting behind the wheel.

She sucked in her breath and nodded, intensely aware of his broad shoulders as he reached behind the seat for the thermos of coffee.

"Going to pout all the way to Wyoming?"

"Maybe."

Suddenly he reached out and brushed her hair back behind her ear, making her start and turn toward him. At that moment he captured her chin with his fingers.

"Look, Beth. I know you don't want to ride back with me. But you're here. Make the best of it." His long fingers moved to the ridge of her jaw, gently stroking, persuading.

She did her best to return his gaze coolly. She wanted to jerk her head away, but she didn't, couldn't.

"I resent your meddling in my personal affairs the way you did," she murmured.

"It got the job done, didn't it? That old battle-ax would've fought every step of the way to keep you."

Beth turned her head to the window. "Every time I speak to Sarah, she assures me she's fine," she said with a worried frown.

"She always says that," he told her. He turned away and started the motor. "But she needs you now."

Interstate 90 was a long straight ribbon of highway running east and west. The flat Minnesota farmland, now frozen and covered with a thick blanket of snow, soon gave way to the equally flat fields of South Dakota. The landscape was broken occasionally by a farm house nestled in a grove of trees, their leafless branches stark and cold. Herds of cattle huddled together in their pens.

At noon they stopped briefly to fill the gas tank, pick up lunch to go, and refill the thermos.

"Can't we stop long enough to eat?" Beth asked irritably after several near spills with a steaming cup of coffee.

"I want to go as far as possible today. The station attendant said a snow storm was brewing over the mountains."

"So what? The highway department keeps the roads plowed."

He smiled, and his mustache twitched. "You're in for a surprise, Florence Nightingale. A Wyoming blizzard is the granddaddy of all blizzards."

"It can't be too different from a Minnesota blizzard," she said stubbornly. "The roads are seldom closed in Minnesota."

"You can't compare Wyoming to Minnesota. Everything in Wyoming is bigger and better. Even the blizzards." His eyes glittered devilishly. His amusement deepened as she tossed him a glare.

"That's a crock!" she told him with a laugh.

"Uh-huh," he said, and kept smiling.

Soon the scenery, as it flew past the windows, started to change ever so slightly, becoming less flat, more hilly, but still with few trees, except around the farms. The towns along the highway were small, few, and far between. Beth knew it would be dangerous to be stranded out here at this time of the year. A person in a stalled car could easily freeze to death.

The truck ate up the miles. The sky changed, turning gray as clouds gathered ahead of them. When it grew darker in the afternoon, Tom switched on the CB radio and the chatter of voices invaded the silence.

"Breaker, breaker—one-nine. Does anyone out there have a copy on this lonesome ol' boy truckin' east? Anyone got their ears on?"

After several seconds another voice answered. "Ten-four, good buddy. I gotcha. You've got the Woodpecker, here. Go ahead."

"Howdy, Woodpecker. Ya got the Red Baron back at-cha. Where'ya headed?"

"All the way to the Big Apple. I've been'a slippin' and slidin' since I left that Shaky Town. Go ahead."

Hoarse laughter crackled over the speaker. "Ten-four."

"This ol' eighteen-wheeler's kept me on my toes, a keepin' her between the ditches. I been all over this concrete ribbon. Rain, sleet, ice, then snow. They've throwed everythin' at me but pretty girls and sunshine. Go ahead."

"I just started my run. I'll take the front door and give a shout if I see those ol' smokies."

"Ten-four, Red Baron. Put the peddle to the metal and we'll be in the Apple in no time a'tall."

"What'cha hauling . . ." The voice faded as they passed out of radio range.

"What's Shaky Town?" Beth asked.

Tom's eyes left the road long enough to meet hers. "That's Los Angeles."

"Oh. What else did he say? I was lost after breaker, breaker."

"Pour me a cup of coffee and I'll tell you."

She passed the hot cup to him after he had negotiated a bend in the highway and passed a slower car. Her fingers touched his and the contact sent warning signals through her. Watch it, she thought. Don't let yourself think of him as anything but Sarah's brother-in-law. Don't forget the heartache of three years ago.

"Almost everyone who uses a CB radio has a radio name, or handle as they call it. A few use the call letters issued to them by the FCC." He shifted in the seat, settling into a more comfortable position.

"Do you have one?"

"Uh-huh."

"Well . . . what is it?" she asked, when he didn't volunteer the information.

"Goat Roper."

"Goat Roper?"

"Yeah. You've got to admit, it's different." Smile lines crinkled the corners of his eyes and he gave her a quirky grin.

Words almost failed her. "If . . . you say so," she said, much too reasonably, and attempted to swallow the laughter that bubbled up.

They lapsed into silence and Tom concentrated on his driving. The loose snow, stirred by brisk winds, made for poor visibility at times. It was easy to be bored with the scenery. It seemed to go on and on without anything to break the monotony.

He must be tired, Beth thought. She had offered to drive earlier, but he refused, saying he knew the highway. Then with a quick glance at her and a twist to his lips, he'd added, "Besides, I don't know what kind of driver you are."

"You thought I was a pretty good driver three years ago," she'd snapped, and then mentally kicked herself for bringing up those days, so long ago, when they'd had such a wonderful time together.

They had stopped only one time since noon, and Beth's stomach was growling with hunger. Tom was tense—she could see it in the way he gripped the steering wheel. It was becoming more and more difficult to see the edge of the pavement.

RAPID CITY. She was barely able to read the sign as they whizzed past.

"We'll stop there," Tom said. "Do you think you can last another twenty miles?"

"I don't know. My stomach is slowly chewing its way to my backbone, and my fanny doesn't feel so good, either." Every bone in her body ached. She wanted something to eat, a hot relaxing bath, and a warm bed, in that order.

"I know the feeling," he replied with a deep chuckle. "I want a gigantic rare steak. We'll get a room, some dinner, and hit the hay."

Tom wheeled the Blazer into the drive of a Holiday Inn just off the interstate. Leaving the motor running, he went into the office. Beth watched him through the window as he signed the register.

"We're set for the night," he said when he slid into the truck.

"Thank goodness."

34

Due to the late hour and the weather, few people were in the dining room when they arrived for dinner. The service was quick and the food good. They ate in silence.

"We're leaving at six in the morning," Tom said when he left her outside her door.

He knocked on her door at five, dressed, packed, and ready to go.

"What time is it, for chrissake?" she asked sleepily.

"Shake a leg. There's a storm warning out." He came into the room carrying his overnight case, his coat slung over his arm. His eyes missed nothing in their quest. They roamed down from the top of her dark tousled hair and sleepy eyes, lingered on her breasts outlined by her blue robe, and moved to her small bare foot. Resentment burned through her, and she stalked to the bathroom.

"I never knew a man who was so consistently early!" she flung at him before slamming the door.

He was standing beside the door, holding her coat, when she came back into the room. She slipped into it, and he turned her gently around to face him. His hands rested on her shoulders, his warm gaze focused on her face.

"Got your long johns on?"

She wanted to say something clever, but could think of nothing, so she nodded mutely.

"Good. The temperature is dropping and it's starting to snow again. We'll be headed right into it.

35

I know you don't want to be stuck out in the boonies, with me." His voice held a smile.

"You're right about that." Her chin was level with his chest. She was too close to him, and drew back. "As long as you're in such a hurry, let's go."

It was snowing hard. Tom unlocked the passenger door, then moved around to the back and loaded their suitcases. The motor started the instant he turned the switch, and while they sat letting the engine warm up, he brought out the thermos.

"This'll thaw you out." He grinned as if he had just pulled a rabbit out of a hat.

"I hope so. Oh, Lordy, it's cold!" She cupped the mug in her mittened hands. The steam from the cup warmed her face, the coffee her insides. "Mmm . . . I needed that." She smiled at him. "Did the tooth fairy leave it?"

"Uh-huh. She left these too." He passed her a cinnamon roll wrapped in waxed paper, then laughed as she attacked it, smearing frosting on her cheeks in the process. He lifted a finger and wiped at her cheek, then stuck the finger in his mouth. "Mmm . . . pretty, and you taste good too." His eyes flicked over her face, studying every contour. Beth felt her body grow tense under his gaze. She almost lost herself in his luminous green eyes, and forgot to eat. A finger on her nose jerked her back to reality. "Your nose is cold. Want a doughnut? They're not as good as the chocolate-covered ones we got that day we went to see the statue of Paul Bunyan and his Blue Ox, but they'll do."

She shook her head in numbed silence. He remembered. Even as he handed her his coffee mug to hold while he drove the Blazer back up the ramp to the interstate, her mind refused to let go of the remark. He'd remembered the trip to Bemidji, and the picnic beside the lake, and the doughnuts they'd bought at a small stand. . . . Every minute of that day had been firmly etched in her memory. She began to shiver, but not from the cold.

The highway was slippery—ice, topped by snow. The sky was full of snowflakes, their density making it difficult to see, although the truck's headlights forged a path into the darkness. Tom expertly maneuvered the truck along the highway, which was starting to dip and sway with the hills. He switched on the CB radio and listened to the truckers discuss the road conditions.

"I'm thinkin' about puttin' ice skates on the eighteen-wheeler," one voice said.

"Ten-four. I'm havin' a problem keepin' the rubber side down."

"Well, you're in for it. I just came from Sheridan and it's bad. Real bad."

"Breaker, breaker," Tom interrupted.

"Go ahead, breaker."

Tom pressed the button on the microphone. "You got the Goat Roper. Can you give me a road report?"

"Which way ya headed?"

"Headed west."

The speaker echoed with non-humorous laughter.

"Lordy, Goat Roper. I've come from there and I've had me a time keepin' this toboggan between the ditches. It's a snowin' and a blowin' clean past the mountains. Go ahead."

"Are they trying to keep the interstate open?"

"They're tryin', but don't know if they can keep it up. I came on at Sheridan. Where're you headed?"

"Cody."

"Keep your eyes peeled, Goat Roper. There's four-wheelers and eighteens sprawled all over the road."

"Ten-four. By the way, what's the handle?"

"You got the Bluebird out of Albert Lea, Minnesota, flyin' back at-cha. That other mean ol' boy is the Beagle out of Red Wing."

"Thanks for the comeback and the info. We'll be heading west with caution. Have a safe trip. Catch you on the rebound. Goat Roper is clear."

"That's a big ten-four, Goat Roper. Have a safe one. You still with me, Beagle?"

"Still got the back door. Just keep on a truckin'."

Tom switched off the radio and gave Beth a quick, concerned glance. "There's a truck stop ahead. We'll stop there for a road check before we go on. Those big trucks can plow through some pretty good drifts."

Beth didn't answer. There was nothing she could say to improve the situation. It was snowing harder now. The wind whipped the white fluff across the road in blinding sheets, causing Tom to slow the truck until they were barely moving. Even with the heater on it was cold in the Blazer, and Beth huddled down inside her coat, trying to keep her teeth from chattering.

"Reach behind you and get the blanket off the rear seat," Tom instructed.

Beth didn't hesitate. She turned to crouch on the console between them and reached for the blanket. Suddenly the truck slid on an icy spot, making Tom jerk the wheel to the right. She was thrown against his shoulder, clutching at the shearling coat to stop her fall. Her hand grabbed at his chest, slipped, and. finally came to rest against his warm neck. She could feel his muscles clench as he worked the steering wheel to stop their slide toward the ditch. The truck bumped to a stop against the snow piled on the shoulder of the highway. He turned his head. Their faces were so close that she could feel his warm breath on her mouth. Silence. Suddenly Beth felt frightened. Frightened that this man would bring her pain, break her heart . . . again.

"You okay?"

She nodded, her thoughts a jungle of confusion. His hand came up to cover hers, warming it, before moving on to brush her cheek lightly. She recovered and moved away, reaching for the elusive blanket. Back in her seat, she covered herself, wrapping the blanket tightly around her legs. Tom reached over and tucked it around her shoulders.

"It's maybe five or six miles to the truck stop. We'll make it."

He got out and cleaned the windshield wipers.

Then, moving slowly, he steered the truck back onto the snow-covered highway. They had not met or passed another vehicle for a long time. It was as if a curtain had been drawn around them, leaving them isolated from the outside world. The truck edged along, the only sounds being the wind and the rhythmic swish of the wipers.

Beth glanced at the man beside her. He was peering intently ahead, trying to see through the driving snow, moving cautiously, in case a car ahead had stalled or slid to the side. His hands gripped the wheel, his strong fingers curled around it. She remembered the feel of his hands on her bare arms, her back, and his fingers curled around her breast when he kissed her. She rushed into speech in an effort to control her runaway thoughts.

"Is it much farther?"

"I don't think so. Although it's hard to see any landmarks." His voice was weary.

Miraculously, the sign indicating the exit to the truck stop was visible. Tom edged the truck onto the shoulder, slowly guiding it off the highway, careful of the ice. They drove down the ramp, slid through the stop sign, but managed to turn onto the highway and drive the remaining hundred yards or so to the truck stop. The parking lot was full. The snow whipped and swirled around, making drifts connecting one vehicle to another. Tom eased in beside one of the huge semi-trucks, its engine still running, creating an eerie cloud of vapor.

It was then that Beth realized she had been holding her breath, and she released it with a long sigh.

Tom echoed her sigh and said, "I wasn't so sure we'd make it."

She looked at him with a smile in her eyes. "I never doubted it for a minute."

"That's because you weren't driving."

"I'm glad I wasn't." She was still smiling.

"So am I." He wiped his fingers across his mustache, then stretched his arms as wide as he could in the confines of the truck. "It's going to be crowded in there, but it'll be warm."

Beth was immensely grateful for the arm across her shoulders that helped propel her to the large restaurant connected to the station. She gripped Tom, her arm around his waist as they struggled to keep their balance on the icy surface of the drive.

The heat hit them as they stepped into the crowded room. Holding onto her mittened hand, Tom threaded his way between tables to a booth near the window. The other half of the booth was occupied by a bearded man in a red wool cap. He moved his coat so they could sit down.

"Been here long?" Tom asked.

"Since this morning." The man answered Tom, but looked at Beth.

She removed her hat and mittens and struggled to get out of her coat. Tom pulled the sleeves from her arms. He stood and shrugged out of his own coat, then made his way through the crowd to the counter.

Beth glanced at the man opposite her, then looked away quickly when she saw him eyeing her speculatively from her head to her breasts, then down to her hand, bare of rings.

"That your man?" he asked softly.

She was saved the necessity of replying by Tom's return.

"The scuttlebutt is that the storm'll blow itself out tonight." He handed Beth a cup of steaming hot chocolate. "I thought you might be getting tired of coffee."

"Thanks. I am." She moved over to make room for him to sit beside her.

"You folks live around here?" The man spoke with a New England accent.

"West of here," Tom said. "You?"

"Boston." He spoke with his eyes on Beth. "Your wife's not used to this weather, is she?"

"I—" A nudge from Tom's knee stopped Beth's denial.

"What makes you ask?" Tom's eyes were sharp and narrow, searching the man's face. He watched the eyes go directly to Beth's left hand.

"No reason. I—"

A commotion at the door caused the man to break off whatever he was going to say. A man had come in supporting a woman. Her head rested against him and blood was running down her face.

"My wife's been hurt!" There was panic in the man's voice.

Beth was on her feet. "Let me out, Thomas." Years of conditioning in the emergency room of the hospital put her into immediate action. She reached the couple quickly. "I'm a nurse. Sit down and let's see about stopping the blood. Thomas, I've got an emergency kit in the truck. Will you get it, please."

CHAPTER THREE

With Beth on one side and her husband on the other, the stunned woman was led through the crowd to the booth. The bearded man got up and Beth pressed her down onto the seat. Bright red blood ran profusely down the woman's face. She was frightened and clutched her husband's hand.

"Is there anything I can do?" The hesitant question came from a young waitress, whose face matched the whiteness of her uniform.

"Bring clean cloths and a pan of water, please. It always looks worse than it is," Beth said to the injured woman as the waitress hurried away.

"I'm all . . . blood!"

"Head wounds bleed a lot. Does your head ache?" Beth examined the long ugly gash on the right side of her forehead.

"No."

"That's good. How about your vision? Are you having trouble focusing?"

"I don't think so."

Beth glanced up. Tom was shouldering his way

through the crowd. He placed the first-aid kit on the table.

"How're you doin'?"

"Okay. I can tape it until she gets to a doctor for some stitches."

"We were barely moving when we hit an icy patch and skidded out of control and headed for the ditch," the husband explained. "She hit her head on the dash when we jerked to a stop. Luckily we were close to the truck stop."

Beth felt in complete control of the situation, relaxed and confident. Her competent hands performed their ministrations, cleaning and soothing at the same time. "Will you get antiseptic and sterile pads from the case, Thomas?"

He placed the articles on the table. "Anything else I can do?"

"Hold your fingers here." She placed his fingers on each side of the wound. "Press the edges together so I can tape them."

His body was curved against hers, his arms encircling her as he reached around to assist her. She was terribly conscious of his warmth and strength as they shared their task.

"Thank you," she murmured when he took his hands away.

"You're most welcome." He smiled into her eyes.

Beth covered the tape with a sterile pad and carefully bound the woman's head with a cloth bandage to hold it in place.

"That'll have to do for now. As soon as you can, see a doctor. You'll need some stitches."

"Thank you, ma'am. We really appreciate it," the anxious husband told her.

"I'm glad I could help." Beth sat down and Tom sat down beside her.

"You'd better get your order in," the waitress said. "From the looks of this crowd, I doubt if the food holds out."

"Thanks for the tip." Tom's smile seemed to fluster the girl. Her eyes sparkled and clung to his. Beth thought she looked like a hungry kid staring in the window of a candy store. They placed their order and the young waitress reluctantly moved away.

The hamburgers and french fries were delicious. Tom ate his and placed another order. While he waited, he helped Beth finish off the fries on her plate. When she laughingly protested, his hand came from the back of the booth and gently tweaked a strand of her hair.

"I'll pay you back," he whispered in her ear.

They smiled into each others eyes and new life began to pump through Beth's tired body. She just barely resisted the temptation to press the length of her thigh closer to the long, muscular one that lay lightly against hers. Usually she could think of something flip to say, but all that came to her mind was how beautiful his eyes were, and she couldn't say that.

The waitress removed the dishes and carefully

wiped the table. Beth was sure the extra service was due more to the teasing smiles and light banter that passed between her and Thomas than to the large tip he'd slipped under his plate after he paid the bill.

The other couple left the booth in search of a telephone. Tom moved his hand to the back of Beth's neck and gently massaged her sore muscles with his fingers.

"Tired?"

"Mmm . . . yes." She knew she should casually lean away from him, but her muscles loved what he was doing. His strong fingers worked magic, playing sensually along her neck, up into her hair, down over the tight cords of her neck. "That feels good," she murmured contentedly.

"You can do the same for me sometime."

He's far too handsome, Beth thought, watching him in the dim light of the restaurant. Her eyes returned again and again to the smooth skin, hard cheekbones, and firm lips beneath the russet brown mustache. Suddenly she felt an inchoate fear of this man, a fear of the completeness she felt when she was with him, a fear that he would become, once again, too important to her. She didn't like the way she was beginning to feel about him. She'd put that schoolgirl crush out of her mind, it was all behind her. His dark lashes lifted and his green eyes locked with hers. His face was so close she could feel his breath, soft and warm on her wet lips.

"Will you?"

"Will I what?"

"Rub my back, little screwball." He chuckled, and the lines in his face shifted. "I think I've almost put you to sleep."

"If you don't stop, I'll fall face first on the table."

"I can't let that happen." He pulled her against him, holding her with his arm around her shoulders. Her stomach tightened with nervous apprehension when his hand forced her head to his shoulder. "This is kind of nice, isn't it?"

"I don't know what you're talking about," she said tightly.

"Silly, foolish, independent little cuss," he whispered with soft amusement in his voice. "Relax and lean on someone for a change. It won't set women's lib back a hundred years if I hold you."

Beth wanted to speak, but her voice seemed to have dried up. Inside her a wild, strange voice shouted a warning. *Be careful!* She was consumed with a variety of emotions—mainly fright, because what she was feeling was so strangely familiar, and regret, because she wasn't sophisticated enough to handle her feelings.

The other couple came back to the booth and settled down to rest much the same as Tom and Beth were doing. The restaurant began to quiet down. Lights were turned down and people dozed. A few of the travelers played cards or talked, their voices subdued.

She felt Tom's breath on her ear before she heard his soft whisper. "Comfortable?"

47

"I'm fine. You?" she whispered back, lifting her head to meet his eyes.

"You don't hear me complaining, do you?"

Her eyes dropped to his mouth. The firm lips under the dark mustache twitched into a grin as he saw her eyes move over his face. The hand that held her moved to cup her upper arm and rub it gently. She could feel his heart beating under the palm of her hand. Their eyes met and Beth felt a strange drowsiness. The warmth of his body against her was making her feel so relaxed that almost against her will, she lowered her head to his chest. His fingers came up to turn her face toward him, then stayed to caress her cheek gently before moving on to her ear.

"You like being a nurse, don't you?"

"Yes, I do."

"You're good at it. You handled things well, little Florence Nightingale.

"I only did what I've been trained to do." His hand on her ear was chasing coherent thought from her mind. In the semidarkness his features were unclear, except for the firm lips stretched over white teeth as he smiled. "I've been trained to handle emergencies, Thomas. I've helped to put many a mangled body back together. You do what you have to do."

"Cool-hand Luke, huh?" There was a definite note of respect in his voice.

For an indeterminate time she was aware of nothing except the scent of a masculine body: a combination of wool, leather, and soap. This was

Thomas. Thomas was here, holding her. She turned her face to soft flannel that pushed against her nose as gentle breathing lifted his chest. She felt each beat of his heart against her cheek. I wonder what kind of patient he'd be? she mused. There's one thing for sure—he'd only have to ring once. The nurses would fall all over each other to take care of him.

"What are you thinking about? What caused the chuckle?"

"I was visualizing you as a patient."

"I'm a good patient."

"I bet! Men, as a rule, are terrible patients. When were you in the hospital?"

He shifted farther down in the seat, taking her with him, holding her firmly, while his other hand moved to pull his fur-lined coat over both of them.

"It was while I was playing football at Oklahoma State. I had knee surgery. Everyone, especially the nurses, made my stay . . . most pleasant."

"I bet they did!"

"There was one who—"

"You don't have to explain. Every hospital has one or two who serve beyond the bounds of duty."

The mustache brushed across her forehead. "Are you one of those?"

She didn't look up. She didn't dare. "A good nurse is firm, efficient, and impersonal."

"Firm, efficient, and impersonal," he echoed. "Sounds dull."

"That would depend."

"On what?"

"On what kind of a patient you are."

"I might try to pull you into bed with me," he said softly, his breath warm and moist on her forehead.

"I know all the correct moves. It would never happen."

"So it's been tried, huh?"

"Several times."

He pulled the coat closer around them, his large shoulder shielding them from the others in the room. Beth's mind was in a spin. Why am I allowing this? Why don't I move away? His fingers caressed her cheek before moving around to trace the outline of her lips. Unconsciously she held her breath as his fingers continued their exploration, stopping to caress her earlobe, then losing themselves in her rich dark hair. He held her head firmly against his shoulder while his mouth dropped to follow the path his fingers had taken. He gently brushed her cheek, his breath coming softly to her parted lips. She felt his lips trace a path, and then he was pressing them against hers. Her hand moved to stroke his cheek, his neck, then fastened tightly to his collar. His kiss was exquisitely gentle, demanding only what she was willing to give in return. It seemed to Beth that the world stood still while she was held close to the broad chest by the brawny arms of this man who had thundered back into her life and turned it upside down again. He deepened the kiss before he raised his head and looked at her.

"No—" she said breathlessly, but the word was muffled by his mouth as it returned to her own.

"Shh . . ." His mouth wandered over her face. "Let me kiss you. We deserve it after what we've been through today."

"No—"

"You're all grown up. . . ."

She didn't know what to make of his words. She hated herself for letting him hold her, kiss her. She meant nothing to him. Nothing.

He stroked her hair, then whispered. "It was a nice ending for our third day together. Go to sleep. It'll be morning soon."

Sleep was the furthest thing from her mind, but as he continued to smooth her hair, she closed her eyes. Her hand gripped his shirt, then relaxed as she fell asleep. Several times she felt him move, seeking a different position to ease his cramped muscles. Each time he cradled her closer against him. She burrowed into the nest made by his arms, giving herself up to the warmth and comfort he provided.

"Wake up." The words were accented by a gentle shake, interrupting Beth's beautiful dream of floating in a warm scented bath.

"Mmm . . ."

"Rise and shine. The bugle blew an hour ago."

Beth's blue eyes, heavy with sleep, opened to a room that was still dim. She saw two buttons, then a chest, topped by a firm chin. One of her arms was wrapped tightly around his waist. She lay partly on top of him, their tangled legs hanging off the end of the seat. Consciousness returned like a slap in the face. She struggled to sit up, pushing herself away from him.

"What time is it?"

"Almost six o'clock. Do you hear anything?"

She cocked her head to one side and listened. "The wind has stopped blowing! When?"

"Several hours ago. The snow plows have gone through."

The intimacy of the night vanished with the early morning light. Beth felt her cheeks redden with his inspection, and quickly excused herself to go to the rest room. She splashed water on her face, brushed her hair, added a touch of makeup, and wished she had her toothbrush.

Get a tight hold on yourself, Beth, old girl, she said silently to her reflection in the mirror. Thomas is not only good to look at, he's tough and wild as a hawk. He thrives on the unconventional and unexpected. He kissed you because he deserved it, like he said. And he thought nothing of holding you in his arms. He held you before and it meant nothing. Haven't you learned a thing?

Feeling ridiculously self-conscious, she went back to the booth and slipped in beside Tom, carefully stashing her purse on the seat between them.

"I ordered your breakfast. Here it is." He smiled at the waitress, an older one this time, but she was no less affected by his charm.

Beth looked with dismay at the stack of toast, the two fried eggs, and several fried sausages.

"I never eat this much!"

"Force yourself. No telling when we'll stop."

With the first bite she realized how hungry she was, and quickly cleaned her plate. She sipped the hot coffee and watched people prepare to leave. The weary travelers were eager to move on. Truck drivers were calmly discussing such things as jackknives and frozen gas lines, while women were bundling up their children for the walk to their cars. The howling wind had stopped, but it was still bitter cold. Beth heard a soft purring noise and wondered what it was. Finally, after several minutes, she asked Tom.

"What's that sound?"

"Diesel engines."

"I never noticed it before."

"You didn't notice it yesterday because of the wind, but they were running even then."

"They ran all night?"

"Sure. They may not start again if they're turned off." He fingered his chin, covered with a brown stubble, and Beth forced her eyes to move away from him. "Also, if they're hauling a special cargo that must be kept at a specific temperature, the engine has to run to maintain the heater or refrigerator on the trailer." He smiled at her. "Make sense?"

"I guess so. I never thought about it."

"Most people don't." He motioned for the waitress to refill their cups.

Just then, the woman with the bandaged head and her husband came to the booth. "We're going," she said, "but we couldn't leave without saying thank you again."

The man shook hands with Tom. "Let me add my thanks too."

"Be sure to see a doctor," Beth urged.

"I will. Bye."

"We'd better get a move on too. Do whatever you have to do while I pay the bill." Tom moved toward the cash register that sat at the end of the counter, pulling on his coat as he went.

Beth went to the rest room again, and when she returned, the restaurant was even more crowded and Tom was nowhere in sight. Thinking he had gone to start the car, she went through the crowd toward the door. Then a voice stopped her.

"Where ya goin', pretty thing? You been here all night?"

Beth looked into the bloodshot eyes of a young man who couldn't have been much more than a teenager. He had a stubble of a beard on his face and a silly grin due, she was sure by the smell of him, to too much liquor. She gave him an icy glance and tried to move by him. The maneuver brought her close to the wall, and before she realized it, she was pinned there by his arm, blocking her way to the door.

"Are ya tryin' to give me the brush-off?" His sour breath assaulted her.

"I'm not trying to give you anything, junior. Bug off!" She tried to dart under his arm, but he moved it downward and stepped closer, so that his body shielded her from the view of the others in the restaurant.

"You ain't goin' to be friendly?" He looked over at two men lounging against the wall. "She ain't gonna be friendly," he announced with mock disbelief, and one of the men laughed.

"Okay, buster. You've had your fun. Get out of my way." Beth spoke in the quiet professional tone she used when talking to an unruly child in the hospital.

"Let 'er go, Harley. She don't wanna play," one of the other men urged.

"Well, I do!" The boy's voice turned ugly, and he moved closer, until his body was against Beth's. She still wasn't frightened. Out of the corner of her eye she could see people passing by and could hear the hum of voices in the restaurant. She brought her arms up between them and pushed.

"You cocky little . . . creep! Get away from me or I'll scream so loud I'll burst your eardrums!"

He stood his ground, as if daring her to open her mouth. When she took a deep breath, his hand flashed out, but before he could touch her he was flung back with such force that he stumbled into a group of truckers on their way to the door.

Tom reached the boy before he could regain his balance, and shoved him against the wall, bouncing his head on the hard surface.

"If you want to play with someone, punk, I'll play." Tom waited, his eyes like bits of hard green glass.

The boy looked up in fright at the angry man towering over him. Finally he scooped up his hat, and with his two friends pulling him along, he hurried out the door.

Beth was astonished at the violence of Tom's attack. She had been confident she could handle the situation. With her back braced against the wall, she could have brought her knee up sharply and rendered the boy helpless, without causing a scene. Her face burned with embarrassment as her eyes swept the sea of staring faces.

Tom reached for her arm and ushered her out the door without saying a word.

CHAPTER FOUR

The cold wrapped Beth in its icy blast as she slipped and slid her way to the parking lot. She had to concentrate on keeping her balance on the frozen surface as well as keeping up with Tom's long strides. He unlocked her door, then moved around to the driver's side.

Beth's temper began to simmer at a low boil. "There was absolutely no need for you to use such a heavy hand against that boy."

Silence.

Tom inched the truck forward until he could see if

the road was clear, then eased it out onto the highway. The plows had pushed the snow into high mounds on each side of the parking lot entrance, making it difficult to see oncoming traffic. Several trucks were already rolling down the ramp to the interstate and Tom pulled in behind them.

"You didn't have to push him into the wall," Beth persisted stubbornly. "You might have caused a concussion."

He gave her a cold glance and then turned his attention back to the highway.

"Thomas!"

"Hush up!"

Had she heard him correctly? she wondered.

He looked at her, read her expression, and repeated the words slowly for emphasis. "Hush up!" His voice was low, toneless, and she heard the anger beneath the surface.

"Why did you—" she began.

"Force is the only language a punk like that understands." The smoldering glance he gave her would have melted an icicle.

"I could have handled him."

"How? By saying 'Oh, please don't!'" He mimicked her voice.

"No. By using a few of the things I learned in a self-defense course."

"You obstinate little mule!"

Beth gave him a withering look. "No more obstinate than you, Mr. Clary."

"I'm sure you've taken care of obnoxious pests before, *Miss* Marshall, but this time there were three of them, and they could have hustled you out the door before you had time to bat your eyes."

"I could have handled it," she said stubbornly, though grudgingly admitted to herself that he was right.

"You think so?" His mouth twitched, but he managed to suppress his smile. "Forget it."

His dismissal of the subject made Beth all the more determined to not let the issue slide by.

"There are ways of dealing with an unpleasant situation without resorting to violence," she said primly.

He shook his head slowly. "You *are* mule-headed!"

Beth refused to take up the challenge of that statement, and turned to stare out the window. She gazed with unseeing eyes at the snow-covered landscape. But this was only a ploy to mask the turbulent emotions churning within her.

Three years ago he had been fun, and charming, and had worn his magic as casually as he did his shearling coat. Now she realized there was a depth to him she had not seen before. A relationship with him would not be an easy one. She sighed deeply. Where was the gentle man who held her in his arms last night?

The altitude was higher as they drove on. Snow covered everything, rounding out sharp angles, giving the trees and boulders a softer appearance.

Evergreen branches hung heavy with the accumulated snow. Dark clouds ahead of them cluttered the gray sky.

"The only thing that could make this weather any more disagreeable would be for the wind to pick up," Tom said drily. "The snow would block the highway in a matter of minutes if it began to drift."

Beth thought over his words for a few minutes. "What about your cattle? How do you feed them in this weather?"

"Most of them are brought in to feeding stations. But for the ones out on open range, we fly the bales of hay out in a small plane and dump them. It's quite a ride." He flexed his shoulders in an attempt to ease his tense muscles.

"What about the horses?"

"They're brought to the homestead in the fall. The mares that are in foal are stabled. The yearlings are quartered in another area of the ranch."

"It's like frontier days."

"Not quite."

"Wouldn't Buffalo Bill be astounded to see hay being dropped from a machine in the sky? Basically, life on the range hasn't changed all that much, according to cowboy movies. Cowboys still need horses to round up cattle and . . . do all that other stuff." She finished with a wave of her hand.

"Tell you what. When we do all that 'other stuff,' you can come along." His eyes were laughing now, his face relaxed. This was the charming side of his personality. With an effort Beth looked away from his starkly masculine profile.

"Have you always lived in Cody?" She needed something sane and sensible to say, something to distract her thoughts.

"Except for my years at college and my stint in the Marines. Both Steven and I grew up like wild Indians." His voice was laced with melancholy. "I was two years younger and four inches taller than Steven. He used to say that I got the legs and he got the brains. We both loved horses, and from the time we could walk, we each had one." He slowed the Blazer and carefully guided it over an icy patch of highway. "We played all the usual pranks on each other while we were growing up. He was my brother, but also my friend."

"You were lucky. It doesn't always work out like that."

"After Steven finished college, he joined the Navy. He wanted to see the world. It seemed like every six months he was transferred to a different part of it. He loved traveling, seeing new things, meeting new people. After my three years in the Marines, I was ready to come back to the ranch. Dad died shortly after that. Mom was shattered, but she's tough. She picked up her life, and now travels—sometimes alone, or with a group. It's worked into a sort of new career for her. She guides tours all over the world. I guess that's where Steven got his wanderlust."

There was a long silence while Beth absorbed this

brief bit of family history. She had always felt a little guilty because she hadn't liked Steven. She didn't really know why, unless it was because he was almost *too* perfect. He was handsome, polished, and polite to the extreme. Sarah had been reluctant to mention Steven since telling her of his death, and Beth wondered if her sister were still grieving. Finally she asked Tom about Steven's accident, because she had never heard the details. Tom seemed uncomfortable, but after much hesitation, he began to speak.

"Steven was driving into Cody when he was killed. A rock slide had partially blocked the highway, and he swerved to avoid it and collided with a truck. It was tough on all of us. Sarah hadn't been feeling well, and about that time tests revealed that she had multiple sclerosis, but she hadn't told anyone. It was a double blow."

Beth was silent. Lord, she thought, first our parents, then Steven, and now this dreadful disease. How had Sarah managed to keep her sanity?

"I still don't understand why she didn't call me. No job is more important to me than my sister. Of course I'd have come to help out. Sarah would have done the same for me."

"I doubt it was just the job that made her decide not to tell you at the time. I remember her saying it had been tough on you to uproot yourself from the family home after your parents died. You had studied hard to get your license and it wasn't fair to upset you."

"I talk to her a couple times a month and she's

never said a word about not feeling well. She tells me she's happy and that she's loved helping you out around the house since Steven died."

"Her condition has stabilized. There's no emergency, as I told you. She doesn't know that I went to Rochester to get you. That's a decision I made on my own. In the first place, I thought that if you were the person Sarah says you are, you'd want to know and want to be with her. In the second place, Sarah needs her family. I think it will make all the difference in her attitude."

"She's had you." She remembered saying that once before. She didn't know why she said it again. Perhaps it had something to do with the deep, quivering breath he had taken when he finished speaking.

"Yes. She's had me." It wasn't a positive admission, and Beth's brows drew together in puzzled thought. "She has good days and bad days. But mainly she needs companionship. She loves her home and it would kill her to have to move to a nursing home to get the care she needs. What better way for her to be able to stay at home than to have her sister, the nurse, with her." He glanced at Beth, then abruptly changed the subject. "It's twenty-five miles to Cody and the ranch is seven miles beyond. We can stop at Cody and stretch our legs."

"It's my fanny that needs the relief. It'll never be the same again."

"Wait until you've spent a day in the saddle," he said with a teasing grin.

The day dragged on. Beth felt as if she had been in the Blazer forever. But it wasn't until her stomach growled and she glanced at her watch that she realized how late in the afternoon it was. The roads were icy, so progress was slow, despite the fact that the traffic had thinned with the coming of evening.

Beth yawned and stretched. "I'm tired, but not as tired as you are, I'm sure." The rhythmic movement of the truck had made her drowsy. She smiled at him when he glanced at her.

"Hot food, a shower and shave, is what I need."

"Funny you should mention that. I was thinking the same thing."

"I didn't know you shaved!"

"Fun-ny!" she countered with an impish grin.

Cody appeared at the end of the long curved highway and stretched out toward the gentle slopes of the mountains. They followed a yellow school bus into town, then turned off the highway. They parked in front of a cafe whose sign boasted the best steak in the Northwest.

"What a trip!" Tom said as he shut off the motor. "My shoulders feel like they've been in a strait-jacket."

Beth watched him. Being tired did nothing to diminish his virility. When he looked at her, his eyes were like the green foam on a turbulent sea. His nose was proud, the shadowed cheeks faintly grooved with fatigue. He was a handsome, powerful man. He caught her look, smiled at her, and reached for his coat.

"Let's get out and stretch our legs."

"Every muscle and bone in my body is protesting," she groaned as she slid from the seat to stand on shaky legs.

"Tom? I thought I recognized that bucket of bolts." The voice came from behind, and a stocky man in a leather coat and stocking cap came toward them from across the parking lot.

"Hi, Pat. How ya doin'?"

"Fine, Tom, fine. Here today, gone tomorrow. You know how the cable business is—go where the business is or go without." His friendly blue eyes matched the wide smile on his face. He looked at Beth and waited, plainly wanting an introduction.

Tom's hand rested on her arm. "Beth, meet Patrick O'Day, a wild Irishman."

"Pleased to meet'cha, me darlin'." He snatched the cap off his head and bowed over her hand. "Don't let this rogue scare ya. I'm Irish, yes . . . but wild, never!"

Beth smiled. It was impossible not to. The man's dark brown hair hung down over his ears, and his cheeks were pink from the cold. But it was his eyes that drew her attention: they were pale blue, and crinkled with smile lines at the corners. He wasn't as massive as Tom, nor as handsome, but he was attractive. He released her hand reluctantly, but held her with his eyes.

"We're going in for a quick bite, Pat," Tom said. "See you around."

"Mind if I join you?" His smiling eyes were on Beth. He didn't see the frown that crossed Tom's face, but Beth did, and she wondered about it.

Pat and Tom were greeted by friends as they followed the waitress to a corner table. The cafe was small and reflected the western atmosphere with checkered tablecloths and a rough plank floor. It had been hours since breakfast, and Beth was hungry. The waitress, dressed in jeans, a plaid shirt and a cowboy hat, took their order.

"Are you a rancher, Mr. O'Day?" Beth asked over the din of western music blaring from the jukebox.

"Pat. Call me Pat." He laughed as he said it. "My company does aerial and underground work, mainly for the telephone company and cable television. It's too cold to work here at this time of year, so I'm heading for warm country."

"When are you leaving?" Tom asked pointedly.

"I'm not sure. It depends." He smiled at Beth with open admiration.

She blushed. "Your work sounds interesting."

"It is. I'll tell you about it over dinner some evening, if the ol' hoss, here, don't have his claim staked."

"Beth's here to take care of her sister, Sarah," Tom informed him flatly.

"Sarah? I wouldn't have guessed you were sisters."

"We're half-sisters, actually. I'm terribly anxious to see her."

"She's had a raw deal." He frowned, then a slow smile spread over his face. "I'm sure you'll have some free time. I'll show you the sights."

"That would be nice of you," Beth said, avoiding Tom's gaze.

"I'll give you a call."

The waitress brought large hamburgers in baskets. The delicious odor wafted up. Beth inhaled deeply and laughed. "Mmm . . . good! I'm starved."

"Didn't the ol' hoss feed you?" The Irishman's eyes were warm on her face.

"Not since breakfast."

"I'd a looked after you better'n that," he said with a caress in his voice.

"Don't blame me, blame the weather. We've had a hell of a trip." From his tone Beth knew that Tom was in no mood for light banter.

"We caught the edge of it," Pat said. "I saw Herb in town yesterday. He said they'd been hauling hay, gettin' ready for the blizzard."

"Herb's a good man. I knew he'd handle things, but I'm glad to be heading home."

"You're damn lucky to have him. I know several ranchers who'd give their right arm to get him away from you."

Tom ate quickly and rose to leave as soon as Beth finished. "Ready?" he asked.

She picked up her purse and glanced at the other man. "It was nice meeting you, Pat."

"My pleasure." He smiled at her as if she were the only woman in the world. "I'll call you," he said softly.

"I'll see you before you leave," Tom told him as he helped Beth into her coat.

"I'm sure you will." He winked openly at Beth.

It was dusk. The sun had moved behind the mountains, casting long shadows over the valley.

"Why the come-on to Pat?" Tom demanded as he eased the truck back onto the highway.

Beth looked at him with disbelief. "What?"

"You heard me. You couldn't have sent the message more clearly if you'd written a letter."

"I didn't give him the come-on. I tried to be nice to him because he's your friend. That's all!" She couldn't believe her ears. He was angry! What was going on? "I was just being—"

"Yeah, I know. You were just being . . . friendly."

He was silent after that. The lights of Cody were left behind as they turned onto a snow-covered gravel road. Tom maneuvered the Blazer expertly, but Beth clutched the door handle as they swung curves and plowed through snow drifts.

Tall, stately pine trees lined the winding road; beyond them were large, open spaces.

"We're almost there." Tom slowed the truck and turned to look at her. "You can let go of the handle now."

"Are you sure?"

"Uh-huh." She heard a chuckle after the grunt.

"This is beautiful country, even covered with snow."

"I love it. I wouldn't live anywhere but here."

"I can understand why." She gazed out the window and caught sight of something in the trees. "I think I saw a deer!"

"Could be. They're thick as fleas. Federal land adjoins mine and they're plentiful."

"They're so beautiful. How could anyone shoot them?"

"If they're not thinned out every so often, they starve. The land can only support so many."

"I know, but those soft brown eyes—"

"You'd have made a lousy pioneer."

"That was different," she argued. "It was kill or go hungry. I could shoot one if my family needed food."

"Have you ever fired a gun?"

"No."

"I'll give you a lesson, in case we ever run out of meat."

"I'm not sure I want a lesson, thank you," she retorted, and hugged herself with her arms.

"You should learn the fundamentals. There may be a time when your life will depend on it."

"All right. But I'm not going to shoot anything."

"God, I hope not. The only thing you'll shoot at is a target."

The road bent to the left, and Tom turned sharply to the right and onto a wide drive. They had been driving parallel to a split-rail fence for a few miles and this drive was the first break. A tall post flanked the drive, and suspended over it was a large wooden sign: GRIZZLY BEAR RANCH.

"I didn't know your ranch had a name."

"My great-grandfather named it."

Evergreen trees lined the lane as it wound back toward the mountain. As the trees began to thin, Beth glimpsed the ranch house. Even from a distance it looked huge. As they drew closer, she saw it was made of logs. It was nestled there as if it were part of the trees and mountains that surrounded it. It was two-storied with a wide covered porch. A gigantic stone chimney rose into the sky at one end of the house and was emitting a trail of smoke. A thick layer of snow covered the roof. Shrubs and bushes were scattered around the yard, but they were almost buried under the snow. There were buildings to the back of the house and to the side. It was a large complex.

The door rose as they approached the garage, and Tom drove the Blazer inside. After switching off the motor and turning on the inside light, he turned and looked at Beth for a long moment. Finally, he spoke.

"You may be surprised when you see Sarah, Beth, but don't let it show. She's not to be upset." He spoke quietly, but his tone conveyed a firm message.

A streak of fear raced through her heart. What did he mean? Oh, Lord! "I'm a professional, Thomas. Even if Sarah *is* my sister, I won't allow my anxiety to show."

"I understand that, but—"

"You don't understand anything about me," she blurted. "How could you? I knew you . . . briefly, a long time ago. And less than a week ago you came bulldozing your way back into my life. You don't know me at all."

"Has it been less than a week?" he asked in a low, husky tone, and swung open the car door.

CHAPTER FIVE

Beth's mind was whirling with conflicting thoughts. She tried to slow her steps, hoping to regain her composure before facing the sister she hadn't seen since so much tragedy had come into her life. Tom's hand was firm on her shoulder as he ushered her toward the house.

"C'mon," he urged impatiently. "I phoned my ranch foreman and he's told Sarah that you're coming."

They went up a couple of steps and into a side entry. Thick rugs were laid out on the tiled floor to soak up the snow carried in on overshoes. After slipping off their boots, they silently removed their coats, and Tom hung them on pegs hanging along the wall.

Beth followed him through a door to the kitchen. A dim light was on over the range, and a big dog stood in the middle of the room, wagging its tail. Tom switched on the ceiling light.

"Hello, girl." The dog came eagerly to him and he fondled her ears. "Where is everyone?"

The house was so quiet, it was eerie. Beth glanced

around the large kitchen. It was equipped with contemporary cabinets and appliances, but set against one wall was an antique sink, complete with a red iron hand pump and filled with plants. In the middle of the room was a round oak table and high-backed chairs. The far end of the room was used for casual living, with a massive fireplace, chairs upholstered in red and white check which matched the wallpaper, and a long, low couch. The room had a warm lived-in feeling.

"What a marvelous kitchen," Beth said, her eyes roaming around the room.

"Efficient too. I had it done to Sarah's specifications. She almost drove the builder nuts."

Tom gave the dog a final pat on the head and straightened up. He was the only familiar thing in the quiet, unfamiliar room, and when he reached out his hand, Beth's went out to meet it. A quote from her father came to mind: "You can trust a man whose eyes smile when he does and who is kind to animals."

The ring of the telephone broke the stillness. Still clutching her hand, Tom reached the wall phone.

"Yeah, Herb."

Beth wondered how he knew who it was, then saw the numbered lights on the phone and realized the ranch had an intercom system. From the look on Tom's face, she knew the news he was getting wasn't good.

"Wasn't that kind of sudden? Why did they decide

that right now, and how in the hell did you get her to the hospital?" he asked in a deadly calm voice. Then, after listening and nodding: "Yes, she's anxious to see Sarah." The green eyes shifted to Beth. "Was Sarah frightened when you got stuck? No? Jean was right to stay with her. How long will she be there? A week or longer. Damn! We'll go see her in the morning. You may have to open up the lane again if the wind comes up. Yeah, Herb. Thanks for watching for me. I was beginning to wonder what happened when no one but Shiloh came to meet me. Things will work out fine now that Beth's here. She'll be able to give Sarah the shots and save her that long, hard trip to town. Yeah . . . bye."

He put down the phone gently and turned to Beth with a worried look. "They took Sarah to the hospital yesterday. Something about a pain in her back. They want to change the medication, try something new."

Oh, Lord! Beth thought wildly. Why didn't he come for me sooner? A flush touched her cheeks as her eyes sought out his face. The message in her features was loud and clear. He knows that I'm not as calm and collected as I pretend to be, she thought, and wondered if he realized he was still gripping her hand.

"How about making coffee?" he suggested gently. "I'll bring in our suitcases."

"The small one has my overnight things. No need to bring in the others. Tomorrow I'll find a room near the hospital."

Tom's expression was enigmatic. He reached behind her and opened a cabinet door.

"The coffee's in here. Do you like waffles? There should be some in the freezer. Pop a few in the toaster. That hamburger we had in town was just an appetizer."

Trying to disguise the nervousness building up within her from the feel of his hand on hers, and the blatant caress of his thumb against her wrist, she blurted angrily, "I think I can handle that."

Tom lounged against the counter, his arms folded, Beth's hand trapped against his chest. She tried to pull it away, but he refused to let go. A slow smile warmed his face. A dark shadow of beard and tired, half-closed eyes were the only indication of the long rough drive he had just finished.

"I bet there isn't much you can't handle when you set your mind to it," he murmured.

"May I have my hand back, or do you plan to keep it permanently?" Her throat was tight and she snapped out the words. She had to get away from him so she could get some control over her mind.

His eyes assessed her critically, moving over the dark, tumbled hair to the blue eyes glinting at him. When his eyes settled on her mouth, her lips trembled at the image that came swiftly to mind: his hungry, probing kiss taking possession of her as she willingly allowed him that possession. His gaze traveled to the firm breasts rounding out the sweater she wore, and he smiled before he lowered his head and planted a quick kiss on her lips. The familiar soft brush of his mustache sent a weakening thrill through her.

"Stop it!" She jerked back angrily.

"Okay," he said good-naturedly. His long body straightened and he stretched his arms in a gesture of tiredness, bringing her up against him. He folded his arms behind her, pinning her arm behind her back.

She tried to move away. Her heart was pounding like a scared rabbit's and she was sure he could feel it beating through her thick sweater.

"Are you out of your mind?" she demanded breathlessly.

"I think so. I'm so damned tired I just might be off my rocker. Aren't you going to offer me a little comfort and try to soothe my frayed nerves?"

"Only if you think a swift kick or a karate chop will help."

He laughed, but she wondered for the hundredth time why she had come here with him. How was she going to be able to avoid him in the days ahead?

Abruptly he released her and moved toward the door. "Make that four waffles and the coffee strong," he told her, knowing full well how he was irritating her.

Beth stared at the closed door and wished desperately that her heart would slow down so she could think clearly. She didn't want to feel anything for him, nothing at all. He was trouble with a capital *T*.

Now her worry over Sarah was making her too vulnerable to cope with him, and she resented it. That accounted for her heart's nervous flutter, she reasoned angrily.

She brushed a hand across her forehead and picked up the coffee maker from the spotless counter.

The dog, Shiloh, stood waiting beside the door for Tom, completely ignoring Beth's presence. Beth was delving into the freezer for the waffles when Tom returned from outdoors. She didn't look at him until she saw her two large cases out of the corner of her eye.

"Thomas!" She followed him to the stairway. "Thomas! I'll only need the little one for tonight."

He walked up the wide carpeted stairway without looking back, and her anger flared. He was the most impossible, domineering person she had ever met. "You'll just have to bring them down again in the morning," she called as he disappeared down a hallway at the top of the stairs.

The big dog followed closely behind Tom. Beth turned back to the kitchen feeling sick and exhausted. She just wasn't prepared for the agony of having to fight him at every turn. "You've got yourself into a sweet stew this time," she muttered. "You haven't had your head screwed on right since you met him."

Tom came downstairs and crossed to the outer door again. Beth turned her back and refused to look at him. She heard him murmur to the dog,

"Watch out for the bear-cat in the kitchen, Shiloh, or she'll bite you."

Beth tightened her face muscles to keep from smiling. She needed to stay angry. It was her only defense against his masculine charm.

Tom made three trips from the garage to the rooms upstairs, and by that time the coffee had brewed and the waffles were ready. She put them on a plate and set it on the end of the counter.

"Aren't you going to eat?"

"I'm not hungry," she snapped.

"Have coffee with me."

"I seldom drink it at night. It keeps me awake."

"You need something. Sit down and I'll make you a cup of chocolate."

"Chocolate has caffeine too. Besides, your waffles will get cold."

"I'll heat them in the microwave. You're just being stubborn again. Sit down."

Beth gave a resigned shake of her head and settled on a padded bar stool at the counter. Minutes later he set a steaming cup before her, with a plump marshmallow floating in the warm foam. It smelled delicious. And the warm hand that lingered on her back when he set down the cup sent ripples of pure pleasure through her.

No words passed between them while he ate his waffles and she sipped her chocolate. When he had cleaned the plate and poured himself a second cup of coffee, he reached over and clasped her hand.

"Go on up and take a good hot bath. I'll clean up down here. One of Sarah's rules—whoever makes a mess in the kitchen cleans it up before they leave it."

"Do you always obey Sarah's rules?" The words sounded caustic, and she wished them back immediately. She felt even worse when he ignored them.

"Your room is the second door to the right."

The bedside lamp was on when she reached the room. She looked around and her eyes lighted with appreciation at the queen-sized bed covered with an intricate tapestry spread. Matching long drapes framed the small-paned windows. The furniture was white French provincial; the lamp shades and a deep, soft chair were covered with a dusty rose fabric.

Beth loved the furnishings. She stood quietly for a long moment and let herself enjoy the unexpected beauty of the spacious room. With a soft, tired sigh, she picked up her cosmetic case and went into the adjoining bath. She filled the tub, poured in a generous amount of fragrant oil, and sank into the warm bath.

Thoughts of Tom tormented her as she lay back and let the warm water ease the tension from her tired body. The memory of the kisses they shared last night had refused to dim during the day. She could close her eyes and feel the soft touch of his lips and the gentle brush of his mustache against her face. Damn! She had been kissed before, even by him. It was the damn mustache then, and it was the damn mustache now! Why had she let him hold her and kiss her? She knew she was playing a dangerous game. My God! Hadn't she learned anything from that disastrous encounter so long ago? He had taken it for granted that his attentions would be welcome. With his good looks, she doubted if he was ever refused. For the first time she wondered if he had a steady woman friend, or a lover. A man of his good looks and virility was bound to seek physical release. His commanding presence and the magnetism of his personality would arouse most women with hardly any effort at seduction on his part.

She tried to turn her thoughts away, but they persistently returned to Tom. She wondered if her surrender to his physical presence satisfied a deep need in her for security through male dominance and possession. Her one affair, while trying to blot Tom from her mind, had left her with the feeling that sex was a frustrating experience, and she had come to terms with the belief that perhaps she was a woman with a low sex drive. Now she was not so sure.

Beth lay in the tub and looked at the ceiling. She could no longer deny that Thomas Clary had only to look at her to set her heart pounding. She had to turn off her feelings for him or he would make her into a docile, mindless robot willing to do and be whatever he wanted her to be. Damn him! Her body had matured along with her mind during the three years since she had believed herself so desperately in love with him, and the intensity of her response to him was proof that her burgeoning needs had been denied too long.

She dried herself with a thick towel, dusted herself generously with powder, and applied a light lotion to her face. Dressed in her pajamas and robe, she padded barefoot into the bedroom and turned back the bed covers.

A soft knock came on the door seconds before it opened. Beth turned in astonishment as Tom casually walked into the room as if they had been living together for years.

"I heard the water pipes gurgle and knew you'd let the water out of the tub," was his only explanation.

"Oh?"

"I've built up the fire in the fireplace. C'mon down and see the rest of the house."

"Thank you, but I really want to get to bed."

"So do I, but I'll wait until we're better acquainted."

"If you're trying to shock me, it won't work. I'm not a trembling child, nor am I frightened because we're alone in the house." She looked at him in the mirror of the dressing table, and saw that he was grinning.

"Thank God for that!" he murmured. "C'mon." He took her hand and pulled her toward the door.

"Stop, Thomas. I don't have any shoes on."

"I noticed. You don't need them. I'll bed you down on the couch and you can tuck them under you."

"You'll . . . what?"

"Poor choice of words. You can sit on the couch and keep your legs tightly together. I promise not to attack you, although . . . I'd certainly like to." His eyes twinkled as her mouth tightened and her nose lifted in defiance. They were at the head of the stairs, and he was two steps below her. She tugged on her hand and he turned. Their eyes were even. "C'mon, or I'll kiss you right here."

"I wish you'd stop playing your adolescent games," she said crossly. "I'm a grown up, professional woman and would appreciate being treated like one."

"You don't look like a professional woman. You look like a scrubbed little kid." His eyes held so much mirth that she had to whip up her resentment to keep from smiling.

"*You* don't look as if *you* were lifted from *Esquire*."

"You noticed? Three minutes in the shower, two minutes to shave, two minutes to jump into my clothes. Seven minutes . . . all for you." A smile tugged at his lips, as if he were completely unaware of her belligerence.

He's flirting with me, she thought, and lifted her hand to brush the thick swath of dark hair from her forehead. His own dark hair was wet and tousled, and the terry shirt he had pulled over his head clung to his damp shoulders. He had on soft, faded jeans and . . . white socks! She wanted to laugh. She hadn't seen a man in white socks in years. His strong male ego needed a setback, she thought, so she did laugh.

"White socks?"

"Sure. I always wear them in my boots." He was totally unperturbed by her amusement. He raised dark brows. "As a nurse, I thought you'd approve. C'mon, your feet will be getting cold."

Beth allowed him to lead her down the stairs and back to the living area in the kitchen.

"I thought you wanted me to see the rest of the house."

"You can see it in the morning." He led her to the couch and pressed her down.

What's the matter with me? she fumed. He's either leading or pushing me into whatever niche he wants me in, and I follow like a Iamb being led to slaughter. She felt a strong desire to jump up and go sit in the high-backed chair opposite the couch. At that instant his eyes met hers.

"Sarah has to have a high, solid chair. It's impossible for her to get up out of low ones without help."

Beth sank back down on the couch. Damn him! He can read my mind. She sucked in her breath and looked around as if concentrating on the room, but she was intensely aware of him moving to the stereo.

"Do you get good television reception out here?" She had to say something; the silence was making her feel ill at ease.

"Are you a TV fan?"

"Not really."

"Sarah is. She loves it. We had the cable run out

here so she could watch a movie any hour of the day or night."

"I've never had the time to become addicted to TV."

"Want to see if there's a good X-rated movie on?"

She knew he was trying to shock her again, and she refused to take the bait. She shrugged indifferently, sorry that the gesture was lost on him. He had turned his back and was fiddling with the controls on the stereo. When the music reached her ears, she jerked her head around in surprise. She didn't know what she had expected, but it certainly wasn't Beethoven's "Moonlight Sonata."

Her eyes sought his and her lips parted in one of the warmest smiles she had given him.

"Do you like that?"

"I love it," she said softly.

"Somehow, I thought you would." He sat down on the couch, leaned his head back, and stretched his long legs out in front of him. "Now, this is my idea of a pleasant evening—a crackling fire, a quiet house, soothing music, and . . ." he rolled his head and faced her, ". . . a pretty woman all ready for bed."

Color flooded her face. His eyes glinted devilishly, his lips twitched in an effort not to laugh. He *was* flirting with her, but it wasn't going to work! She'd had male patients who had tried to jar her out of her calm reserve, but she had never had to try as hard as she was now to keep her composure.

His hand snaked out and grabbed hers. "I'll stop

teasing you. You're too tired tonight, and it's no fun unless you fight back. Come over here beside me and stretch your feet out to the fire. I'm enjoying this even if you're not."

"No—"

"Yes." His arms pulled her over against him. "Now, isn't this better? Relax. You're stiff as a poker." He reached down and straightened her legs, then lifted her bare feet and rested them on one of his jean-clad legs. His arm encircled her and he pressed her head down onto his shoulder. "Ah . . . you smell good and feel better." He buried his nose in her hair. "Just like ol' married folks, sittin' in front of the fire when the chores are done and the kids in bed."

"Thomas—"

"Mmm . . . ? If you've got anything to say, you'd better say it now, because I'm going to have to kiss you in a minute."

"Now look! You work too fast for me. I've only known you—"

"Three years and five days and four nights. I didn't sleep a wink one of those nights. I didn't want to miss out on a minute of the time your tight little body was pressed to mine. Did I tell you that your little bottom is a nice handful?"

"Stop it, Thomas!"

He let out a bellow of laughter. "God, I love it when you get your back up!"

"Enjoy yourself while you can. I'm going into town tomorrow. I'll stay at the hotel. I'll spend my days with Sarah as her private nurse. If she's not coming back for a week or two, there's no need for me to stay here."

"There's every need for you to stay right where you are."

Beth sat back and closed her eyes. I won't argue the point with him now, she thought. She tried to relax, but everything about him—his physical attraction, his personality—made that impossible. She wondered if he could feel her insides trembling. She tried to ignore the warm hand that slid up the loose sleeve of her robe to stroke her arm with long slow movements. His head moved, his breath fanned her mouth, and her eyes flew open.

Amusement, curiosity, and surprise all mingled in his eyes as he looked at her. "You're trying awfully hard to stay ramrod stiff and not enjoy this. Loosen up. I haven't raped a woman in over a week now!" His tone was teasing.

She put her hand on his chest to push him away, but it was like pushing against a mountain. Her lips tightened and she kept them that way even as he covered them with his. Oh, God, she prayed, help me to hold out against him.

"Eliz-a-beth." His lips left her for an instant, and his tone was cajoling. "Beth." His voice was a mere whisper against her mouth. "Your lips are as tight as a miser's purse. Let me in."

"No. Thomas—"

"Yes . . ." His fingers were pushing her hair behind

her ears as his mouth silenced her protest. "Mmm . . ." The sound came from his throat, and his arms locked her to him.

Beth had not imagined such an assault on her senses. She wanted to surrender to the excitement of his touch, her mouth responding to the insistent persuasion of his. The kiss deepened. His hunger seemed insatiable and his caress became savage, his skilled sensuality blotting out everything but his power over her senses.

"Beth . . . Beth, your mouth is so . . . sweet," he whispered, his lips moving to her eyes. "You were sweet before . . . but now . . ." The soft feel of his mustache on her face drove her into a frenzy of need, and she lifted her fingertips to his cheek and pulled his mouth back to hers. He responded instantly to the urgency of her desire. His tongue gently stroked her inner lips, the moist, velvet texture sending spasms of delight down her spine. She drove away any thoughts that might shadow the bliss of the moment.

He lightened the pressure of his mouth so that their lips were touching gently. "Soft, sweet, delicious. I had forgotten your mouth tasted like this." His voice was no louder than a sigh.

Her arm slid around his neck. She was drowning in sensuality. A sweet, unbearable, erotic pleasure-pain had started in the pit of her stomach and spread to her womb with throbbing arousal. She gently worked her fingertips between his mouth and her cheek and stroked the soft hair above his lip.

"Do you like it, sweet?" The words were breathed between nibbles on her fingers.

"I love it."

She angled her head so that their noses were side by side and rubbed her face against his mouth. She heard a soft sound come from his throat and felt the trembling in his body, as he buried his face against her neck. His hand had burrowed inside the robe and under the top of her pajamas. Softly, gently, he first cupped, then stroked her breast, fitting it into his palm, his thumb resting on the swollen nipple. When he pressed her down onto the couch with gentle insistence, Beth's desire raged war with her instinct that this was a dangerous game she was playing.

"Thomas . . . we shouldn't—"

"I know we shouldn't. It's too soon for you. I'm trying hard not to grab you and take you upstairs to my bed. I want to love you all night long . . . I wanted to last night—" His lips covered hers very lightly, his tongue caressing the edge of her mouth. "I want to love you very gently, until you ache for more."

CHAPTER SIX

Beth knew she should stop this headlong flight into sensuous pleasure, but the weight of Tom's body pinned hers to the couch and played havoc with her desire to escape. Her fingers caressed his thick hair. His mouth nuzzled her throat, then moved slowly lower to explore the breast his hand had exposed.

Emotions, long dormant, surged uncontrollably through her when she felt his tongue caress her nipple. She stifled the desire to cry out when his lips, then teeth, nipped lightly at it.

"Please, Thomas . . . we must stop!"

Suddenly a cold, wet nose thrust against her face. She moved her head to the side to evade the dog's tongue. Tom raised his head and was immediately accosted by the insistent animal, who whined, then barked for attention.

"Dammit, Shiloh, what is it?" he said thickly. The dog continued to bark, her tail swishing rapidly from side to side. Then she jumped up and down and ran toward the back foyer.

"I think she needs to go outside," Beth suggested.

Outside was the magic word: it sent the big red dog into a frenzy of barking. She raced to the door and back again to thrust her nose into Tom's face.

"All right, Shiloh, but your timing is lousy!"

Tom's fingers lingered on Beth's exposed breast, then gently pulled her robe together and buttoned it. He eased himself up to lean over her, and his fingers played with the curve of her jaw.

"Saved by the dog," he teased. "And she isn't even a Saint Bernard."

Strong currents of embarrassment kept Beth from looking at him. He'd wanted to make love to her, and . . . *bang,* just like that, she'd been a pushover! Oh, Lord! *I've never been so stupid in all my life,* she thought wildly.

"C'mon, dog. I may just feed you to the bears," Tom said to the dog on his way to the door.

Beth heard the outside door open and scrambled to her feet, hurrying up the stairs to the sanctuary of her room. She closed the door and leaned against it. Tom was a man familiar with seduction. Even with her lack of experience, she knew that only too well. Fighting back the feeling that she had made an utter fool of herself, she sat down on the edge of the bed. The lamp cast a warm glow in the room. She flipped it off and slid beneath the bedcovers. When a door closed downstairs, a quick surge of blood sent her heart galloping. She heard the dog come bounding up the steps, followed by the even tread of the man who had turned her emotions into such a riot of confusion that her seriously ill sister was taking second place in her thoughts. She held her breath as his footsteps neared her door.

"Good night," he called. "If the road conditions permit, we'll go into town in the morning to see Sarah. Okay?"

"Okay," she replied. She exhaled the long breath she had been holding. I've lost control, she thought, moaned softly, and turned on her stomach, clutching the pillow. His very presence is more than I can handle right now. Her face burned with embarrassment as she thought of how she had welcomed the intimate touch of his hands. It hadn't taken much at all, and she was panting in his arms. "Ohh . . ." She burrowed her head deeper into the pillow, trying to erase the image of his face from her mind's eye. Finally she turned and stared into the darkness until she slid into a fitful sleep that held dreams of green eyes and sensual lips beneath a soft curve of mustache.

Beth opened her eyes to a gray room. The sun was concealed behind rolling clouds, and the wind, whipping around the corners of the house, caught and held the tall pines in its icy grip, tipping them back and forth with its force. Loose snow fell against the windows and piled in the corners, making a Christmas-card scene. She didn't want to leave the warm bed, but forced herself to throw back the covers and stumble to the bathroom on legs stiff from the long ride in the truck. She splashed cold water on her face and scanned her reflection in the mirror. She didn't look any different, she thought. But then, how was an idiot supposed to look? She did feel better about the situation this morning, so she told the face looking back at her: you've been a pushover. Just chalk it up to being overtired and let it go at that.

She dressed in navy wool slacks and a white turtleneck topped with a Norwegian ski sweater, her Christmas gift to herself last year, and went downstairs. The kitchen was empty, but the radio was on and a voice was giving the weather report. She poured a cup of coffee and sat on a bar stool to listen. The detailed weather report didn't sound good. More snow was in the forecast along with high winds. Oh, that's just great! she thought. More snow, more wind. Just what we need.

The door opened and Shiloh raced in. Her paws were covered with snow. She stopped in the middle of the room to shake, then bounded over to Beth, nuzzling her arm and almost upsetting the coffee cup in her hand.

"Hold it, girl," she said, laughing and eased the cup of sloshing liquid to the counter. She reached for the dog's ears and rubbed gently. Tom was leaning against the doorjamb. She knew he was there, but she refused to look any higher than his stockinged feet while she petted the dog. Out of the corner of her eye she saw the feet approach the counter, and then they were planted firmly as he sat down on a bar stool.

"How about scratching my ears?"

She glanced up. A smile lifted his mustache, and she lowered her eyes to the dog.

"If I did anything to your ears it would be box them." She hadn't meant the retort to be humorous, but he laughed, and after a while, so did she.

Tom reached over and took a sip of her coffee. He was warmly dressed for the outdoors. Snow dusted his shoulders and she could smell the cold air that permeated his clothing.

"Well, what's the verdict? Can we make it to town?" Beth was instantly proud of her calm voice.

"Sure. If we get stuck, Herb will come with the tractor."

"Okay. Give me a few minutes to get my things together."

"There's no need. I'm thinking that as long as you're here, the doctor will let Sarah come home. This is where she wants to be."

Beth stood and moved to the door leading to the stairs. "But what if he won't allow her to come home?" The question hung in the air.

"Then we'll consider what's the next best thing to do."

A thoughtful frown covered her face as she went up the stairs. What did he have in mind? With determination in her every move, she packed her overnight case, and without giving herself time to wonder what Tom would say when she appeared with case in hand, went back downstairs.

She could hear a motor running out on the driveway and Shiloh's frenzied barking. She put on her snowboots, heavy coat, and pulled a wool stocking cap down over her ears. The blast of cold air almost took her breath when she opened the outside door. Her eyes watered and she turned her back to the wind as she hurried to the Blazer parked in the drive. A cloud of vapor from the exhaust rose and was scattered by the force of the wind.

Before she could open the door, something hit her on the back. She half turned, and—*bang,* a snowball whizzed by, missed her, and flattened against the side of the truck. Sheltered by the Blazer, she turned and looked back to see Tom and Shiloh romping in the snow. He was wearing an orange insulated jacket and a blue stocking cap. As she watched, he scooped up another handful of snow and formed it into a ball. She opened the door at the same time he launched the missile. The snowball went through the open door, hit the window on the driver's side of the car and smashed, filling the seat with snow.

Beth jumped in and slammed the door, giggling, and fervently hoping the heater would melt the snow and leave a wet puddle in his seat.

"Coward! Come out and fight!" he yelled.

Beth put her thumbs in her ears, wiggled her fingers, and stuck out her tongue. Seconds later a snowball smashed against the window. Thinking he had to be part Eskimo to stand the frigid cold, she watched him play with the dog. Then, with the dog nipping at his heels, he walked across the drive to talk to a man on a huge green tractor with a snowplow attached to the front.

By the time he opened the door to the Blazer, the snow in the seat had melted, but Beth had forgotten about it until he took a towel from beneath the seat and wiped it dry.

Tom's green eyes twinkled at her. Cold had reddened his cheeks and a fine film of snow lay on his head and shoulders. He radiated health and vitality.

"Brat! Why didn't you wipe off my seat?" he grumbled.

"Why should I? You threw the snowball."

His grin was wicked. "Brave, aren't you? Just you

wait, my girl. You've got one coming." He removed his gloves and picked up the microphone to the CB. "Breaker, breaker, Geronimo. Got a copy on the Goat Roper?"

"I gotcha, go ahead." The voice that barreled in on the speaker was so loud that Beth flinched.

Tom turned down the volume. "Ten-four. Keep your ears on, we may need you to come pull us out of a drift. The Goat Roper and the Little Mule are headed for Cody." He signed off and hung up the mike. He was grinning devilishly. "Fits, doesn't it? And to think, I just now thought of it."

"Brilliant. You must be very proud." Beth was trying to maintain her cool reserve and was failing miserably. Her lips were pressed tightly to keep from smiling, but her bright blue eyes flashed him an amused look.

The east-west road was clogged with drifting snow. The tractor had cut a path, but it was apparent that the swath would be filled in again soon. The blowing snow made for poor visibility, and Tom sat hunched over the wheel, concentrating on his driving. Beth didn't speak until they reached the highway and turned south.

"Who is Geronimo?"

"Herb, my foreman." Tom sat back and relaxed. Traveling with the wind at their back made for easier going.

"Does he live at the ranch?"

"We have two tenant houses. Actually we have

three, but one isn't in use now. Herb lives in one and my head stockman and his wife Jean live in the other. Jean has been helping out at the house and went into town with Sarah. Herb was divorced about five or six years ago. His wife longed for the bright lights and went back to Denver. That wasn't their only problem, I guess, but it was the major one. Herb misses his daughter and makes several trips a year to see her. She spends some time here with him in the summer."

"Does the daughter share the mother's fondness for the bright lights?"

"Lord, no! Susan's a long-legged twelve-year-old in love with her horse. She's a real sweet kid," he said, cautiously swinging the truck around a stalled car. "If her mother wasn't such a bitch, she'd let her stay here with Herb, but then she'd lose the generous child-support payment."

"You sound bitter."

"I am. You'd be, too, if you could see how happy that kid is while she's here and how she looks like a little whipped pup when she has to leave."

"You like kids?" Beth stared at him suspiciously. There were many facets to this unpredictable man's character, and this was a new one.

"Sure, don't you?" He gave her a searching look, then his voice deepened to what sounded like a growl. "Don't tell me that you're one of those career women who don't like kids."

"I didn't say that. Of course I like children. I plan to have some . . . someday. That is if—"

"Some?" he cut in.

"More than one," she snapped.

"Why are we quarreling? I want that too." He smiled, and there was a mischievous glint in his eyes.

She started to contradict him, then, remembering how he enjoyed raising her hackles, she forced an indifferent shrug. His small chuckle told her he had read her mind, and she decided she'd rather die under torture than give him the satisfaction of knowing how he affected her.

Speechless now, she leaned back in the seat and tried to ignore him. From the corner of her eye she caught his sideways glance at her, but she stubbornly looked straight ahead.

"Are you warm enough?" he asked abruptly, turning the louvers on the hot-air vents. A waft of warm air flowed over her.

"Sure. I'm fine," she said stiffly.

"How come you've not married? Were you waiting to snag a rich doctor?"

This time she let herself look at him, her eyes following the clear-cut line of his set profile.

"Why do you ask?" She fumed for a moment, waiting for him to reply, and when he said nothing, she rushed into speech. "I haven't married because I haven't found the right man. Not that it's any business of yours. When I marry, if I ever do, it will be forever. My kids will not be shuffled back and forth between divorced parents."

"My sentiments exactly."

"Furthermore, here's a small bit of news for you to file away for future conversations when you feel inclined to pry: I don't indulge in casual relationships."

"You sound pretty bitter," he said. His eyes clung to her face for as long as it was safe before looking back at the road. "What happened? Did you have an unhappy love affair? Did someone jilt you?"

"No!" she said quickly, cutting him off. He mustn't know that it was her old feelings for him she was thinking of. "I don't want to talk about this anymore. Forget it, will you?"

"Sure," he said with a shrug. "That's the hospital ahead."

The sidewalks were ice-covered, and the wind biting cold. Beth walked beside Tom into the brick and glass building, his hand firmly grasping her elbow. He stopped at the information desk to ask for Sarah's room number, spoke to several people, then ushered her to the elevator. This was familiar territory to Beth. Hospitals always smell the same, she mused. Her nurse's training shoved her mind into its professional channel and her anxiety about seeing Sarah was overshadowed by her desire to speak to the attending doctor and get a detailed report on her sister's condition.

The door of the room was ajar when they reached it. Tom stepped back so she could enter the room alone. She steeled herself to expect the worse, and pushed open the door.

Sarah, in a maroon robe, was sitting in a chair beside the window, a paperback novel in her hand. Her blond hair was swept up and pinned loosely at the top on her head, exposing her long slender neck. She looked beautiful and fragile.

"Elizabeth! Oh, darling, I'm so glad to see you!" She held out her arms and Beth went to her with tears clouding her vision. She leaned over and kissed her sister, then grasped her hands and stood back to look at her. Sarah was thinner; it was evident in the lines at the sides of her mouth, in the skin on her neck, and in her slender wrists.

"You silly, crazy woman!" Beth exclaimed. "I'm so angry at you I . . . could beat you! Why in the world didn't you tell me about this?"

Tears now flooded Sarah's eyes. "I didn't want to worry you. I've never really been a part of your life, not that it was anyone's fault. At first I was angry at Thomas when Herb told me he'd gone to Rochester to get you; then, selfish woman that I am, I was glad, and have been counting the hours until you got here."

"You should have known that I'd want to come and be with you." She returned her sister's teary smile. "I'm sure I can get a job right here in this hospital, and I can see you often."

"Oh, Beth, I'm so glad you're here. I wanted you to come but I didn't want to interfere." Tears rolled from her violet eyes. "Now that our parents are gone, there's only the two of us left."

Beth released Sarah's hands and took off her coat.

"Yes, and how foolish we've been to live so many miles apart. There was really nothing to keep me in Rochester except my job."

"Where's Thomas? That man is stubborn as a mule. He has a one-track mind, and for months it's been on getting you out here."

Beth smiled. "I'd say he was more mule-headed than stubborn."

"I heard that." Tom's big frame filled the doorway. "Are you two ganging up on me?"

"Eavesdropping?" Beth said brightly.

"Sure." He dropped a kiss on Sarah's forehead. "Why not? How ya doin', sweetheart?" His gaze was honed in on Sarah's face and his voice was full of loving concern.

"I'm all right," Sarah said firmly. "Now, why did you bring my little sister out in this blizzard? Don't you know there's a travelers' warning out, and this town is full to overflowing with busloads of people they've taken off the highways?" She shook her head, but gazed at him affectionately. "Sometimes you and Herb don't have a lick of sense. You both need a keeper."

Tom's eyes went from Sarah to Beth. "You two are more alike than I thought. You're both bossy."

"I'm not!" The denial came out sharply, and Beth wondered again why this man's teasing could prick at her and make her so angry so quickly.

"Now, I can't have the two people I love the most quarreling," Sarah said. "You'll have to learn to ignore him, Beth. He loves to tease, especially if he thinks he's getting under your skin."

"That's easy for you to say," Beth said, eyeing Tom, who leaned nonchalantly against the wall, watching her so intently that butterflies began to flutter in her stomach. "Sometimes he's as hard to ignore as that blizzard out there."

"Speaking of the blizzard, I don't think you two should stay in town very long. The last report was that they're pulling the snowplows off the highway." Sarah's worried eyes flicked from one to the other. "As much as I'd enjoy a long visit with you, darling, I'll feel more comfortable when I know you're safely at home."

"I'm staying here." Beth didn't have the courage to look at Tom. "I'll get a room nearby. You'll have your own private nurse. How about that?"

"Oh, dear. I'm afraid that isn't possible." Sarah looked at Tom for confirmation. "I doubt if there's a vacant room to be had in town. You don't know how it is here at a time like this. The town will be filled to the brim. Motorists, skiers, hunters . . . all will be stranded here until the storm is over. You'd best go back with Thomas. He'll take care of you."

"I brought my overnight case and a uniform." Did she hear Tom swear under his breath? she wondered, and turned slightly, so that his face was out of her line of vision. "I want to speak with your doctor, Sarah. There's a chance I can stay right here in the nurses' quarters temporarily. Or—"

"Stubborn!" The word sounded grating, issued through clenched teeth.

Beth ignored him. "How about the room Jean is using? She came into town with you yesterday, didn't she? No doubt she'll want to go back home with . . . him." She tilted her head toward Tom, but didn't look at him.

Sarah's eyes bounced from one to the other. "Jean's staying with her mother. She'll be disappointed to have her visit cut short, but I suppose—"

"Beth's going back with me," Tom said firmly.

"Some women may like an arrogant, forceful man, but I'm not one of them," she snapped. "I make my own decisions. I want to see Sarah's doctor, I want to know if there's a position available here for me, and I want to assure him—"

"Beth . . ." Sarah said quietly.

Beth turned and saw the distressed look on her sister's pale face. "I'm sorry, Sarah. I just want to be with you."

"Sarah will need you when she comes home, which will be as soon as the storm lets up," Tom informed her. "Dr. Morrison told me so this morning. He'll give you complete instructions at that time."

Beth turned on him. "You talked to her doctor this morning? Why didn't you tell me?" With an effort she kept her voice under control.

"If you remember, we didn't have much time to talk. You slept in and didn't even have time for breakfast. Is that why you're so cranky?"

"We were together all the way to town!" Beth reminded him furiously.

"We were talking about other things."

When he grinned at her, she let loose with a swear word. It slipped out before she could hold it back.

"Ladies don't swear." He was laughing, and it fanned her anger.

"Ohh . . ." She thought of several things she wanted to say, but Sarah was shifting uncomfortably in her chair.

Tom leaned against the wall, his hands in his pockets, his dark hair ruffled from the wool cap he'd been wearing earlier. His eyes glinted when he looked at her, but softened when he watched the worried expressions flit across Sarah's face. He moved away from the wall and squatted down on his heels beside her chair.

"Herb and I will come and get you just as soon as we think we can make it in the station wagon. Herb said he had quite a time getting you here and said a flat no when I suggested bringing you home today. You won't mind staying a few more days if you know Beth's waiting at home, will you?"

Beth listened with shocked surprise at the wonderfully patient way he spoke to her sister.

"Don't you think I could go home in the truck, Thomas?" Sarah's hands had come up to his shoulders, and her long slender fingers smoothed the hair at the back of his neck.

"And force Jean to cut short her visit?" he chided gently.

"Oh, that's right. But, darling, I'll worry until I know you and Beth are home. Will you call me?"

"Sure. I called this morning, didn't I?"

Beth felt like she was eavesdropping on an intimate conversation. Tom treated her sister as if she were the most precious thing in the world—treated her more like a lover than a sister-in-law.

"Yes, and you got here before I had time to worry." Sarah raised soft, loving eyes to Beth. "This is the most dependable man in the world, and I love him dearly." She reached for her hand. "I want you two to be friends, like you were when he came to the wedding."

Beth was silent.

"For once she's speechless, Sarah. I'll have to remember that line and use it when I want to shut her up."

"Darling, stop teasing her." Sarah looked at him with such a radiant expression that Beth knew her sister did indeed love him, but with what kind of love? "Life doesn't stand still around this one long enough for it to be dull, Beth," Sarah said, while Beth shifted from foot to foot, uncomfortable with her thoughts.

Tom rose. "We'd better get going. Herb will be waiting for us at the turnoff. That east-west road will be drifted shut for sure."

Sarah held tightly to Beth's hand. "I'm the luckiest

woman in the world," she said softly, her eyes misty with tears. "I've two of the most wonderful men in the world taking care of me, and now you, darling. I'll be home soon. Oh, Thomas, won't we have a wonderful Christmas with Beth with us?"

"You bet, Queeny. We'll have the best ever. I'll put in an order for a truckload of mistletoe." His laughing green eyes flashed a look at Beth's face, and she prayed the heat she felt wasn't reflected there.

"Queeny?" she said sarcastically, wanting him to know she thought the nickname ridiculous.

"Thomas and Herb call me that. They tell me that I'm queen of the hive." Sarah's small laugh was nervous, and she gazed fondly at Tom. "If you'll help me out of this chair, love, I'll walk down the hall with you." With his hand beneath her arms, he lifted her to her feet. "The most aggravating thing about MS is getting up out of a low chair," Sarah confided when she was standing. "Thomas fixed my chairs at home so I can get up easily."

Sarah walked confidently, with no sign of the staggering gait characteristic of the disease. Beth's experienced eye noticed this, and she felt a degree of relief that the illness had not yet progressed to that stage. Sarah was taller than Beth and very slender. Where Beth was considered attractive, Sarah was considered arrestingly beautiful, with her fine-boned face, and skin like porcelain. She walked between Beth and Tom as they went down the corridor to the elevator.

"What do you think of the house? Thomas let me remodel and decorate a couple of years ago. I love it. Of course, I liked the cottage too," she added hastily, then explained. "Steven and I lived in one of the cottages. After he was gone, Thomas insisted that I move up to the house."

"It's beautiful," Beth murmured. She felt trapped, and her heart started thudding unpleasantly.

"Call when you get home," Sarah said anxiously.

"Worrywart!" Thomas accused, and kissed her cheek.

The elevator door opened, and Beth gave her sister a quick kiss. Tom held the door so she could enter, then it closed, blotting out the sight of Sarah's gently smiling face.

CHAPTER SEVEN

Snow was falling thick and fast. Whipped by a brisk wind, it swirled around the truck like a thick fog.

"I'll have to leave the window open a crack until the defroster can take over," Tom said. His words were the first spoken since they got in the truck.

Beth stole a glance at him and told herself that she was ten times a fool for being here with him—for going back to the ranch where they would be alone in the house for no telling how long. It was intimidating—he knew exactly what he wanted and how to go about getting it. He was the most controlled person she'd ever met. Even when he had thrown the boy against the wall at the truck stop, his fury had been controlled. He was extremely capable, and according to Sarah, dependable. It was disgusting, she decided irritably, for one man to have so many admirable qualities.

Knowing he was fully occupied maneuvering the Blazer through the dense, blowing snow, she watched his hands on the wheel. Beth felt a shivery thrill remembering those hands moving over her bare flesh, gliding, caressing; strong hands that could crush or be exquisitely gentle. Damn! Damn! She'd better get that thought out of her head. Is he in love with Sarah? Is she in love with him? The unwelcome thought stumbled on the heels of the first one. Sarah was only a few years older than Tom, and it was logical that he could fall in love with his brother's widow.

The truck stopped, but Beth, lost in thought, was unaware of it.

"Don't be afraid. We'll make it okay." His hand left the wheel and lightly squeezed her mittened ones.

"I'm not afraid," she said absently, and something inside her trembled. "I was only thinking."

Tom guided the truck around a stalled car. "What about?"

"Nothing . . . everything . . ."

"Everything?" he echoed. "Sarah will be just as she is for a long time. They don't expect her to get any worse, but no better, either. As you know, MS is unpredictable and affects people differently. Sarah is one of the lucky ones."

"Yes, I know." She stared at him helplessly, cold to the heart. Better to let him think she was worrying about Sarah than to let him know her mind was on *him*.

They were moving slowly, the Blazer plowing through the drifts building across the deserted highway. When Tom blindly reached for the mike attached to the CB radio, Beth picked it up and placed it in his hand. He turned quickly when their fingers touched and gazed at her. His eyes held hers for a timeless second before he looked away.

"Breaker, breaker, Geronimo. Have you got your ears on?" He waited and repeated the call. There was no answer. He handed the microphone back to Beth. "We're not close enough for Herb to pick us up." He looked at his watch. "I told him we'd be back about noon. It's after that now. It's slower going than I thought it would be."

The motor strained when they went through a drift, and the wind buffeted the truck. It was a scary white world, and Beth was extremely glad that Tom was there with her.

"Talk to me Beth." The sound of her name coming from his lips made her heart lurch. She was trying to think of something to say when, to her utter amazement, he began to sing in a low, controlled voice. "I'll take you home again, Kathleen. Across the ocean wild and wide. To where your heart has ever been, since first you were my blushing bride. . . ."

His voice washed over her as if his hands were caressing her skin. Reverberations echoed up and down her spine. A longing to snuggle close to him and have the words he was singing hold a real meaning slowly enveloped her. She tried to shake off the sensation and looked straight ahead, conscious that he turned to look at her often as he sang.

When he finished, she clapped her mittened hands in silent applause. "Bravo! You sing beautifully." She knew her face was flushed and her voice weak. She tried to disguise it with a small cough.

"I've got all sorts of hidden talents." He laughed, and the small wrinkles appeared at the corners of his eyes. "I can make biscuits, sew up a rip in my jeans, use the plunger when the plumbing clogs, and I can . . . can tomatoes."

"Bully for you! You'll make someone a lovely wife someday! Hey—look out!"

Tom saw the small foreign car stalled on the highway at the same time Beth did, and put on the brakes. Although they were moving slowly, he couldn't stop the truck. They slid into the car and pushed it into a snowbank beside the road.

Beth gave a small cry as she was flung forward, only to be held back by the steely strength of Tom's arm as it shot out to hold her.

"Sonofabitch!" The word exploded from him. "Why in hell didn't they push that thing off the highway?"

As he spoke, the doors of the small car opened simultaneously, making it look like a small bug with big ears. Two men got out. They wore sweaters and insulated vests but their heads and hands were bare. Tom cursed again as they hurried to the truck. He rolled down the window and the cold wind blew snow into his face.

"Man, are we glad to see you. We damn near froze to death." The man who spoke was young. He peered into the truck. "Will you give us a ride into Cody?"

"No," Tom said flatly. "I'm not going back. But I can't leave you out here, either. Get in. I'll take you to my place."

"We'll pay, man. We want to get to Cody." A second face appeared beside the first. Both faces were red with cold, both needed a shave, and both had shifty eyes that swept over Beth, then scanned the back of the Blazer.

"I'm not going back, take it or leave it. You can come to my place or stay here and freeze to death. The choice is yours, but make it quick."

"You're not giving us much choice, mister. We'll go with you. We'll get our things from the car."

Tom rolled up the window.

"I don't like them," Beth said quickly.

"I don't either." Tom reached across to open the glove compartment. He took out a small pistol and slipped it into his pocket.

"Do you think—" she began, eyeing the gun with apprehension.

"I don't know what to think. It's best to be sure." He swore again when he saw the men coming back. Each carried a cloth dufflebag, and one had a rifle.

Tom rolled down the window on Beth's side. "Hold it! You don't get into my truck with an uncased gun."

"Holy jumpin' hell, man! We don't have a case, and it'll be snatched if we leave it in the car."

"All right. Hand it in, butt first." Tom drew the gun into the car, checked to see if it was loaded—it was. He ejected the shells, then with the butt on the floor of the truck he leaned the barrel toward Beth. "Hold onto it," he instructed, then to the men, "Okay, get in." He leaned forward to release the back of Beth's seat. The men squeezed behind her and into the back of the Blazer.

She could feel their eyes boring into the back of her head. She turned sideways in the seat so that she was facing Tom. At least she could shout a warning if they made a move toward him. And she would do something, although she wasn't sure what it would be. After glancing at them, she decided they were in no condition to do much to anyone. Both men were shaking from the cold and rubbing their hands together and blowing on them. Their faces were not far from frostbite.

Tom was driving in the middle of the highway now. Occasionally Beth could see the white line where the wind had cleared the snow. They passed another stalled vehicle. One of the men remarked that they had passed it before they had stalled and that it was empty.

"Breaker, breaker, Geronimo—" Tom had called almost continually for the last few miles.

"Ten-four. I got ya." The voice that came back was faint and crackly.

"We'll be there in a few minutes."

"Ten-four. I'll be watchin'."

Tom handed the mike to Beth. "Call him again in a little bit, honey. From now on I've got to watch for the turnoff."

Honey! He had said it naturally, as if it were an endearment he used all the time. She strived to close her heart against the thrill, and took the mike from his warm fingers.

"That's neat!" the younger of the two men said. "You ain't takin' no chances, are ya, mister?"

"A man's a fool to risk more than he has to in this country," Tom said drily.

"I'm Mike Cotter. This here's Jerry Lewis." His laugh was more like a sly snicker. "He's not the movie star, but he's kind of funny sometimes." He snickered again.

A quick glance told Beth that Jerry Lewis didn't think it funny at all. He had a scowl on his face. "This your wife?"

Tom didn't answer, and the man lapsed into silence. When Tom spoke it was to her.

"Give Herb a call, honey."

There it was again! She glanced at him this time. He wasn't teasing her. His brows were drawn together in serious concentration. As she watched, she saw him glance into the rearview mirror. He's keepin an eye on those two, she thought. He doesn't trust them any more than I do. She pressed the button and spoke into the mike.

"Breaker, breaker, Geronimo—"

"Ya got me—" the voice boomed.

"There he is. Dammit, I went past him." Tom braked to a halt, backed the truck, and cautiously turned onto the graveled road.

"Okay, let's go." Herb's voice boomed.

The big, green machine moved through the snow banks, the V-shaped blades making a path. Tom stayed a reasonable distance behind because several times Herb had to back up and make a second run at a drift before he could make a path for the truck.

"Who's in the bunkhouse, Herb?"

"Frosty and John. Gus and Smitty stayed at the line shack."

"I've got two more for the bunkhouse. We'll drop them off there before we go to the house."

"Got-cha."

Tom pulled up behind the tractor when it stopped. The snow was blowing so hard that Beth could just barely see the outline of the buildings. Tom put on his stocking cap and gloves.

"Here's where you get out, fellows." He nodded to Beth to open her door, then unhooked her seat and waited for the men to squeeze out from behind her. The younger man reached for the rifle.

"Leave the gun," Tom said curtly. "You can take it when you leave."

"God, man! You're sure as hell one suspicious cuss." This came from the man called Jerry.

"You're damn right, mack. And I'm alive to prove it. You can wait out the storm here, but understand one thing—you play by my rules. Now grab your gear and follow me."

In seconds the three were out of sight. Alone, Beth slumped in the seat. A trembly sigh escaped her lips. She hadn't realized she was so tense. A new awareness of Tom dominated her thoughts. He was definitely a man of contrasts. She thought of him—tender, affectionate, his eyes warm with loving concern for her sister. That was the kind of man she had dreamed of loving. Then, there was the hard, unfeeling, cold-eyed man who'd grabbed the cowboy in the restaurant and sent him spinning into the wall. She shivered at the thought. Violence was repugnant to her and had become increasingly so during the time she had spent in the emergency ward at the hospital. She had seen the results of violent behavior—battered women and children, gunshot cases, fights— Could she love a man capable of such actions?

Love? Oh, for crying out loud! She had gotten over her love, if you could call a girlish crush love, for this man a long while ago. She was attracted to him, and yes, she wanted him physically. There was no disgrace in *that*. She was a healthy, adult woman. Not that she would jump into bed with him just to satisfy her sexual desires, she told herself firmly. Her dream had been to meet someone, become friends first and then lovers, building a solid foundation for their future together. Then, *bang!* He had come back into her life, and she wasn't sure she was strong enough to resist him.

The day went quickly. After Tom called the hospital and they both spoke to Sarah, assuring her that they had arrived home safely, Beth made sandwiches from the leftovers in the refrigerator and heated a can of soup.

"Herb'll be in to eat with us tonight." Tom was stepping into an insulated snowsuit. "Do you think you can rustle up enough grub for two hungry men?"

"Sure. You're not the only one with hidden talents. What time? And what about the other men? Who cooks for them?"

"Jean cooks when she's here. But they won't go hungry. There's a kitchen and supplies in the bunkhouse. They can manage." He pulled on a ski mask and raised the lower part of it so that it fit his head like a stocking cap. Shiloh was waiting expectantly. "Not this time, girl. We'll be going on the snowmobiles, and there's no room for you. Stay here and keep Beth company." He turned to face her. "I'll call you from the barn if we'll be later than six."

She nodded. "Don't forget your gloves." She picked them up off the counter and handed them to him.

His fingers caught and held hers. "I like having you

in the house, Beth," he told her quietly. "I like knowing that you'll be here when I come back."

She didn't know what to say. She felt a strange slackness in the pit of her stomach. Her eyes were drawn to his, and she was moved by the tenderness she saw there.

"It's . . . dangerous going out in a blizzard. I hope you know what you're doing," she said calmly, proud of the steadiness of her voice.

"I do. That's why Herb and I are going together. We'll take two machines and follow the fence line. We'll be okay." He was still holding onto her fingers, and now he pulled her closer.

"Hey, I've got dishes to do," she protested weakly.

"This won't take ten seconds."

His fingers slid up under her hair at the nape of her neck. He bent his head, without any appearance of haste, and his lips tingled over hers. Her eyes closed slowly. Then, horrified by her lack of resistance, she opened them.

"Do you want chicken or steak for dinner?" she murmured.

"Surprise me. I think you'll find everything you need in the freezer and the pantry."

"Okay." Beth wondered why she felt so faint. The swimming sensation in her head couldn't be caused by his touch alone. The hand behind her head was holding her firmly, and she couldn't move if she wanted to. Liar, her common sense whispered; he's not holding your feet!

"I want to kiss you again." His voice was a rough, seductive whisper.

Shock held her silent for a moment, then she swallowed. "Well, get on with it. I've got dishes to do," she said at last, trying to smile scornfully.

His fingers moved around to her chin and he held it with his thumb and forefinger. He kissed her again, more deeply, his lips clinging, seeming not to want to leave. The kiss was soft and agonizingly sweet and tender.

"You taste like a peanut butter and jelly sandwich," he whispered. Their eyes locked in a silent duel. She was determined to not look away or he would know how his kiss had shaken her.

"Strange, considering I just ate a peanut butter and jelly sandwich." She spoke as lightly as she could and was pleased there was no tremor in her voice.

"Amazing." He gave her a lazy, amused smile.

She wished he would go. She wanted to be alone, to give her mind time to recover its balance. He reached behind him and opened the door. Only then did she step away from him. I've got to keep it light, she warned herself. Let him think casual kisses are the norm with me.

"Amazing," he said again.

It took every ounce of her will to tilt her head saucily and quip in a slightly breathless voice, "Maybe I'll be invited to appear on 'That's Incredible'."

"Not without me, you won't." He stepped backward through the door, and just before he closed it, he said, "Think about it."

She did. Minutes passed while her mind grappled with answers to the questions flooding it. What did he mean, amazing? What were her feelings . . . his feelings? Was it purely physical gratification he wanted . . . she wanted? Dammit! Why was her stupid heart beating so violently? Cripes! I need a bath and two aspirin.

Later, Beth decided she liked being alone in the house. A hot bath and aspirin calmed her nerves and brought out the practical side of her nature. She resisted putting on the blue velour lounging suit that flattered her slim figure and made her complexion look so peachy, and dressed instead in worn jeans and an off-white turtleneck sweater.

While in the tub she had decided to make Swiss steak and mashed potatoes for dinner. The only question was how much to cook. Would it take more than one potato to fill a hungry man? I'll cook two each, she decided. Whoever heard a man complain about too much food?

The foreman was a surprise. Beth had visualized Herb as being older, perhaps middle-aged. He was a man in his middle or late thirties, a large man with brooding dark eyes, black hair, and sharply etched features that proclaimed an Indian heritage. Tom introduced them. Beth smiled and nodded. Herb acknowledged the introduction solemnly.

"It smells good in here. I hope you've cooked enough." Tom caught her eyes and grinned.

"That I can't guarantee, but there must be food here to feed half of Custer's army."

Halfway through the meal the phone rang. Tom's long arm reached for it.

"Hi, Sarah. How'er ya doin', hon?" His smile was beautiful; there was no other way for Beth to describe it. "We're doin' all right. Now you stop worryin', hear? Yes, Herb's here too. And yes, I'll see that he doesn't take any chances in the blizzard. But, hon, he's a big boy now!"

Herb had stopped eating and was watching Tom. His dark brows were drawn together expectantly.

"Yeah," Tom was saying into the phone. "I hope she's a better nurse than she is a cook! Okay, okay—I won't tease her." He shoved the phone in Beth's hand.

"Don't mind him, Elizabeth," Sarah said. "He takes some getting use to."

"He doesn't bother me in the least. I've discovered he's got an inflated ego and that he's all *blow* and no *go!*" She could barely hear Sarah's words over Tom's whoop of laughter.

"It sounds like you're having fun. I wish I were there with you," Sarah said wistfully.

"I wish you were too. Before you come home I'll need to consult with your doctor."

"I've already told him about my sister, the nurse. He's anxious to meet you," Sarah said. "My nurse is here frowning at me. Do you suppose I could speak to Herb for a moment? I'll call you again in the morning."

"Sure. Have a good night. Here's Herb." Beth held out the phone and the big man got to his feet.

He turned his back to the table while he spoke to Sarah. "The weather isn't as bad as the news makes out, Sarah. Tom and I went down to the line shack and everythin's fine. No, I'll stay in the room over the garage tonight." He listened patiently, his shoulders hunched, his dark head bent. "I'm goin' to have to start callin' you worrywart." His chuckle was low and affectionate.

Beth looked up to see Tom's eyes on her. Were both of these men in love with her sister or was it an unromantic love they felt for her because she was beautiful and fragile and inspired their protective instincts?

"Now, Sarah, turn that mind of yours off and have a good rest. We'll bring you home just as soon as the roads clear. Okay? Yes, me too. Bye now." Herb hung up the phone and sat down. "She's always afraid we'll get lost in the blizzard," he said with a worried frown.

"It happened to one of our neighbors a couple of years ago," Tom explained. "He got lost between the house and the barn and froze to death. Ever since that happened, Sarah's been panicky during a storm."

"There's a very real danger. It happens a couple of times a year in Minnesota." Beth refilled their coffee cups.

"That's right. You're from the cold country too." She thought. Herb's voice was soft for such a large man.

"I'm no stranger to blizzards. I hope you two like peach cobbler. That's what you're having for dessert."

"Sit down, honey. I'll get it." Tom lifted the plates from the table and took them to the sink.

Herb took away the empty serving dishes. I can't believe this, Beth thought, and sank back into her chair. They grow a different breed of man out here in the West. She felt a momentary flash of envy when she thought of their gentle concern for Sarah, then instantly regretted her jealousy. Her sister deserved every good thing she could get out of life.

Swiftly and efficiently the men cleared the table and served the dessert. Afterward, Tom filled the dishwasher while Beth stored the leftovers in the refrigerator.

"Is there anything you can't do?" she asked when Tom whipped off the tablecloth and set in its place a wooden bowl filled with huge pinecones.

"A few things, I guess. But I'll try anything once, and some things several times before I give up on them." His laugh was low and sensuous, and a brief shiver ran along her nerves. "Go on, sit down and watch the news. I'll finish up in here."

Beth sat at one end of the sofa with her feet tucked under her. Tom came and sat at the other end. She saw him watching her quietly. Something in his eyes seemed to draw her into their mysterious depths before she managed to look away.

An hour passed. Lost in her own thoughts Beth had no awareness of time. The pictures flickered across the screen, the actor's voice soft in the quiet room. She glanced at Herb. He sat in Sarah's chair, his head resting against the back, his eyes closed, his long legs stretched out in front of him. Tom was equally relaxed, although he seemed to be watching the screen with half-closed eyes.

Beth felt totally at peace before the crackling fire. She was trying to stifle a yawn when Herb rose to his feet and stretched.

"I think I'll turn in before I fall asleep in the chair. Thanks for the supper."

Beth unfolded her legs and stretched them out in front of her to allow the blood to circulate. As soon as Herb left the room, she stood. Before she could say anything or move away, Tom grabbed her hand and tugged. She flopped back down on the sofa and was immediately cocooned in his arms.

"Tom—"

"Ssh!" He pulled her head to his shoulder.

"Don't—"

"That word isn't in my vocabulary, and I don't want it in yours, either." His dark face was adamant, his lean jaw set and firm.

Through blurry eyes she saw his lips nearing hers, and felt powerless to turn away.

CHAPTER EIGHT

Beth was in the most tormented quandary of her life. She didn't understand the part of her that snuggled in Tom's arms and eagerly lifted her lips for his kiss. What had happened to her all of a sudden to wash away her resolve? She didn't want to get involved with him again. But his mouth was incredibly sweet as it closed over hers, gently forcing her lips apart. His arms, unlike his lips, were unyielding and determined around her. Feeling desire curl in her stomach, and the exquisite ache that throbbed in the core of her femininity, she fought desperately to keep her senses. *This must stop!* She tried to turn her face away from his, but he caught her lower lip gently between his teeth and refused to allow her mouth to leave his. When she ceased to resist, he moved his lips over hers, stroking, touching, playing lightly; and then, in what seemed like a pleasurable eternity, he deepened the kiss. Her fingers, seeking the warmth of his skin, moved to his throat and the pulse that beat so rapidly there.

When the kiss ended, she stared at him with glazed eyes. Desire misted her vision and she failed to see the tenderness in his eyes. She tried to hide her aroused emotions with pretended anger.

"May I go now?" she demanded.

"Are you sure you want to?"

She looked at him for a long while. Obviously she

was losing her mind, and what little she had left he could read like a book. Never had it been like this. What she had felt for him three years ago was puppy love compared to this. She longed with all her heart to lift her hands to his face, hold his cheeks in her palms, let her thumbs trace the contours of his lips and her fingertips feel the softness of his hair.

"I'm not going to sleep with you." The words tumbled from her trembling lips. Her breath quickened and her insides were a turmoil of sensations. As she spoke, his arms fell away from her.

"Is that what you think?" he asked with a queer, unfamiliar huskiness to his voice. "You think I'm angling for a quick lay?"

"Well?"

"If it happens between us, it happens, Elizabeth. We're adults, and neither of us is so naive that we don't realize we're physically attracted to one another." He slipped his hand down her arm and interlaced his fingers with hers.

"It's too soon! I don't— I'm not—" The feeling that she was strangling began to grow in her.

"I'll never hurt you, darlin'."

She wanted to speak, wanted to ask him to give her time to get used to the wild, wanton desire that swept over her when she was with him. He was almost a stranger, yet so dearly familiar. She knew he fulfilled everything she wanted in a man. She had instinctively known it three years ago.

"I'm not a man who takes, darlin' Elizabeth." He made no attempt to conceal the yearning in his eyes or the vulnerable expression on his face. "My woman will share with me all the joy of our coming together."

Swimming in a pool of confusion and desire, Beth felt the silence that followed his words wrap around her. *His woman!* Tom studied her quietly and then released her hand. It wasn't at all what she wanted him to do.

"Thomas?"

"Not until you're sure it's what you want, Beth."

Her stomach twisted in a knot. Why couldn't she lean forward and wrap her arms around him? That would be answer enough for him. But she couldn't do it. She couldn't make the first move. Slowly and carefully she got to her feet. She was beginning to realize with increasing force that she wanted more than anything in the world to have his hands run over the most intimate and sensitive parts of her body, to have him look at her with love in the depths of his compelling green eyes. Reason waged war with the hunger that gnawed at her. She wasn't ready for a casual affair with him. There had to be commitment first. It was as simple as that.

"Good night." Her eyes were haunted and dark with despair.

"Good night, Beth." For an instant the mesmeric eyes held her in a thick embrace, then she walked unsteadily from the room.

• • •

Beth woke from a sound sleep and peered into the darkness, trying to read the digital clock on the table beside the bed.

Blackness.

She rolled over and stuck her hand out, groped blindly for the edge of the table and found it. The room was icy cold. She shivered and felt along the table until her fingers found the lamp switch. The click failed to produce the light she expected. The electric power was off. While trying to decide if she should stay in the warm bed or wake Tom, she heard a door close downstairs. Not stopping to think about it, she threw back the covers and reached for her flannel robe. The cold penetrated the robe—her body was chilled and her teeth began to chatter. She felt her way along the wall to the door.

The hall was equally as dark. She stood for a moment, then saw a faint beam of light downstairs. Had someone broken into the house? *The men from the stalled car!* The thought flashed through her mind with the force of lightning.

"Thomas!" Her voice was almost a squeak. "Thomas!" This time her call was loud and carried with it a hint of panic.

The beam from the flashlight traveled up the stairs.

"I'm down here, Beth. The electricity is off. Stay where you are and I'll come up." Tom talked while he moved up the steps. "This happens every once in a while. Usually our rural electrical system is reliable, but that's a pretty strong wind out there tonight. Were you frightened?" He kept the beam of light focused on the floor even when he reached her.

"Maybe a little. What do you do about heat?"

"I've built up the fire in the fireplace. It'll have to do until we get the power back to run the furnace. We've got a generator that will keep the heat tapes on the water pipes going, and the water pump running. *Whoof!*" He made a blowing sound. "You can see your breath in here already. Do you want to go back to bed or come down to the fire?"

"I'll . . . come down."

Beth began to shiver, and it was only partially due to the cold. A quick glance told her Tom was wearing pajama bottoms, and an unbuttoned flannel shirt was all that covered his torso. His hand, wrapped firmly around her side, was meant to guide her down the darkened stairway, but it had the effect of a potent stimulant and her breath started to come in jerky little gasps. She took several deep breaths in an attempt to calm herself.

A fire was blazing in the fireplace, and she moved away from him and went to kneel in front of the blaze and hold her hands out to its warmth.

"It doesn't take long for the house to cool off." She forced herself to speak. When there was no answer, she turned and saw the beam of the flashlight at the end of the room. Then she heard a door close, and Tom came back to her with an armful of blankets. He turned off the flashlight and draped one of the blankets around her shoulders.

"Thank you. That feels good."

"This only happens during a severe storm. I don't remember it happening at all last year." He sat down on the floor beside her and rested his back against a big square ottoman. The firelight flickered over his tousled hair, his face, and down over the mat of hair that covered his chest. He seemed immune to the cold.

Desire, that elusive, unfamiliar feeling she had felt last night and again earlier this evening, spread over her. His eyes held hers in a sensuous embrace, and without being conscious of it, she swayed toward him. His arms opened, then closed around her. She was safely ensconced against his firm, warm chest. She felt the sigh that went through him before she heard it.

"This feels good," he said, echoing the words she spoke earlier, but with a different meaning. His arms exerted just enough pressure to lift her so he could settle his long legs, knees slightly bent, on each side of her. The blanket had fallen from between them, and now he spread it out to cover them. Beth was conscious of the masculine part of him pressed tightly to her hipbone. "When I grow too old to dream I'll have this to remember. . . ." he sang softly in her ear.

"You sing very well."

"Thank you. Now be still and relax. I'll get you warm."

Relax? How could she relax when the primal push she felt inside her was sending her reeling into a world of sensation? Enthralled by his nearness and the effect of his masculinity, she wasn't sure of anything but the force of the sexual awareness that throbbed between them. He lifted a hand to brush her hair away from her face, tucking the silky strands behind her ear. He stroked her cheek before his fingers moved to her throat. Beth was entranced, having lost all touch with rational thinking. She tipped her head, her eyes seeking then losing themselves in his. Her fingers spread and her palm rubbed in a circular motion against the rough hair on his chest. He seemed to be as mesmerized by her as she was by him. It was as if the world had fallen away, leaving only the two of them.

Tom searched the depths of her gaze as she explored his. And then, slowly, he lowered his head until his lips were a fraction of an inch from hers. The sweet scent of his breath, the tangy smell of his skin, and the firm warm flesh beneath her hand were like a powerful drug that started a craving for fulfillment deep in the center of her being.

A small sigh forced itself from between her lips, and her hand slid up to his throat, then to the back of his neck. Her defenses were down. The core of passion that had long lain dormant flared into life, and driven by desire, strong and pure, she fastened her lips to his.

Tom welcomed her kiss with a response so strong

that he trembled. The arm that held her to him was rock hard, and the strong fingers behind her head held it so he could deepen the kiss. Beth quivered at the heady invasion of his mouth and ran the tip of her tongue along the sharp edge of his teeth in welcome.

Somewhere along the way she realized that the pressure of her hand at the back of his neck was no longer needed, and she let it slide, palm down, over the curve of his shoulder and down to the taut flesh beneath his shirt. His skin was warm and hard. Her fingers savored the firmness and discovered little areas that quivered beneath her touch.

"Darlin'." He spoke thickly, his breath coming in uneven gasps that matched hers.

It took Beth a minute to recover from the trance of arousal. Slowly she opened her eyes. His face was so near she could feel the movement of his eyelashes against her cheek. His hand began slowly to smooth the robe from her shoulders.

"Let me feel your breasts against me, sweetheart. . . ." The tenderness of his tone caused a wild, sweet singing in her heart. His mouth moved over hers, soft and then hard. She felt the tremor that shook him when the softness of her breasts touched the hair-roughened skin of his chest. She closed her eyes again as he pressed her hips against the rock-hard part of his body that had sprung to life during their kiss.

"Sex has got to mean something for me," she gasped. "I just can't do it for desire alone!" Her body was a total contradiction to her words. Her arms circled his waist and she moved intimately against his arousal with a tormented sigh. "Oh, Thomas—"

"Don't think about it, darlin'. We may be desperately in love—I don't know. I only know that I've never felt like this before, and I think I'll die if I can't feel every inch of you against me. I want to feel you surrounding me, wanting me. Pretend that you love me, darlin'. Just for a few hours pretend you love me more than anything, that I'm the center of your world and you're the center of mine."

The emotional plea echoed in the far depths of her heart, bringing a mistiness to her eyes and a tightness to her throat. Her arms tightened protectively around him and her innermost thoughts leaped to her lips.

"I don't have to pretend. More than anything I want to make love with you. I love you. I've always loved you. You fill my heart, my thoughts, make my world a joyous place. I'm here, I'm yours—"

"Oh, love . . . oh, my sweet love . . ." His answer was a groan that came from deep inside him.

Beth knew without doubt that she would remember the look in his eyes until the day she died. The expression she saw there was more than gratitude for the gift of sex. It was as if he had waited all his life for something precious, and at last it had been given to him.

Her hands yearned to touch his face, and they did. Her palms pressed his beard-roughened cheeks. When she leaned back, the blanket fell away. The chill was momentary. His hands, work-hardened, moved to cup the gentle fullness of her breasts in a reverent and tender way.

"I love you." A soft whisper came from the lips touching hers. They were three very familiar words, but now she believed them, because she wanted to believe them and because she was beyond thinking or feeling anything except rising passion and building need.

Without further words or thought, in lazy, loving movements, they lay down on the rug beside the fire and he slid the clothing from her body and his. He covered her with his male body and pulled the blanket up over his bare back. Resting on his elbows, his chest barely touching her breasts, he smiled down at her.

"You're beautiful." His voice was low, soft, dreamy. He seemed to be savoring each minute, each second.

"So are you." Her hands drifted over his back in exploration of the curving muscles, sought the indention of his spine, and followed it to taut hips that she pulled against her thigh.

"I want to love you slowly . . . if I can. I want to remember every sensation, every look, every whisper. Tell me what you told me before. I want to see your eyes when you say it." His eyes were aglow with love and desire.

"I love you. You mean everything to me." Oh, dear God! she thought. I mean every word of it. I really do, and he thinks it's pretend! She grasped the smooth hard flesh of his hips and held him to her.

"Beautiful, beautiful Elizabeth. A beautiful name for a beautiful woman." His mouth opened against hers and his urgent tongue sought and found the sweetness of hers. Beth's heart stopped, then sprinted into a mad gallop. "I love you," he whispered against her cheek. "I love you," he whispered against her mouth.

Oh, yes, I believe you! her thoughts spoke silently to him. For tonight, I believe you. The long, lean, muscular body moved over hers. There was no awkwardness, no hesitation. Her arms lifted to slide around his shoulders, and his hands burrowed beneath to lift her up to mold the soft contours of her body to his. It was all so natural. There was no waiting. They became one both emotionally and physically. She felt his weight pressing down on her, and she opened to meet him. With one long, slow drive he filled her emptiness. They were complete and they sensed it at the same time.

"Darlin' . . . how we fit, darlin', how we fit! Oh, woman, you were made for me, and I'll never let you go." The green eyes burned with exultation.

She closed lovingly around him, feeling not only her sensations, but his. She arched toward him instinctively, but he was the master, moving slowly and deliberately, prolonging every single bit of the wondrous heaven as if it had to last a lifetime. Beth didn't need his hands to guide her; she knew what he wanted her to do, just as he knew what she needed.

Together they journeyed to the top of the precipice and beyond, soaring into space in a brilliant blaze of rapture. Together they drifted slowly back through a glowing haze of passion.

Neither of them moved for a long moment, giving their hearts and lungs time to regain their natural rhythms. Beth could feel the tiny aftershocks of climax in the heated sheath that enclosed him. His taut muscles loosened, his head sank onto the floor, and his lips touched the spot beneath her ear. They lay still, sharing the sweet aftermath of fulfillment, bodies still joined, drugged by sensuous pleasure.

"Am I too heavy for you?" A soft whisper.

"No."

"I'm glad. I don't want to leave you." He flicked the line of her jaw teasingly with the tip of his tongue.

"I'm not fragile. I like you there." She circled his shoulders with her arms and turned her face to his. Their lips met in a long, tender kiss while she shifted her legs slightly to cradle his hips more comfortably between her thighs.

Tom lifted his upper body and supported it by both elbows. There was a seeking look in his eyes. "Beth?" Her name was a murmured, husky whisper. "Elizabeth . . . sweet . . . ?"

She knew what he wanted to know. "Unbelievable. How can I describe it?" she whispered. "Beautiful . . . a whole new world. Oh, Thomas—I never knew it could be like that." Her words came softly in marvelous discovery. She caught her breath as his face was transformed with love and laughter. If she didn't know better, she would have thought the glistening she saw in the brilliant green eyes was caused by tears.

His lips moved to hers. Gently and tenderly he held them captive in a long, lingering, trembling kiss. Tendrils of delight wound all through her body and a delicious tickling began to build deep in the part of her that surrounded him. When he would have moved his lips away, she followed with her own, and his sigh was a mingling of pleasure and need.

Tearing his lips free, he murmured, "Darlin', darlin'," and shifted his position to roll on his side, taking her with him. He reached for the back of her knee and pulled her thigh up over his hip, holding her there.

Beth's heart was beating fast, like a trapped bird under her breast. The delicious tickle increased, and she pressed her breasts into the soft hair on his chest. They began to move together with the smoothness of velvet. His hands were everywhere: on her back, her breasts, pressing against her hips. Her breath came in short gasps as they moved together, fitted and welded, while the light from the flickering fire poured over them.

Then came the moment when they stopped moving and simply clung, winging through space into a new and glorious heaven. It was as if skyrockets were bursting inside her, cruising through her veins, tingling in her scalp and down to her toes. She gripped him, wanting it to go on forever, partaking of his love in a whirl of wonder. *This was love!* This was the strongest emotion in the world. It held everything together. It was what poets wrote about. She had not understood it before. It was bliss, to have his body linked to her body, his heart beating against her heart!

Beth lay curled in his arms, and even as they rested, their lips sought and their hands soothed. It was so peaceful, this blessed togetherness. She was sated, filled with the wonder of her newfound sensuality. Tom nuzzled her neck, holding her close. She could sense that he didn't want to leave her, and it made her love him all the more.

"I've got to put more wood on the fire."

"I know."

"I don't want to move." His hand glided down her back, exerting just enough pressure to mold the full length of her naked body more tightly to his.

"You can come back." Her lips were parted against the warm smooth skin of his neck. She sucked on it gently and caressed it with the tip of her tongue.

"It's almost daylight. Herb will be coming in soon."

"Oh!" Mortified, Beth pulled away from him and reached for her gown.

Tom laughed softly. "Don't worry, honey. He'll have to come through the garage, and I threw the inside bolts. I don't exactly trust the two we picked up today."

The fire was only burning embers now, and in the dim light Beth saw the gleam of Tom's naked body as he stood to slide into his pajama bottom and shirt. Would her life ever be the same after this night? She had not realized the bliss, the oneness that could be felt with another human being. It was as if she had become an extension of him, would forever be an extension of him. Her eyes devoured him as he bent to place the logs on the grate. What were his intentions now that they had shared the most intimate act that can be shared between two people?

Beth wrapped her robe tightly around her and sat on the couch. Tom poked at the fire until the logs caught, blazed, and crackled, then turned his back to it and looked at her. She couldn't see the expression on his face, and a quick spear of fear pierced her. What was he thinking? Did he think this was the norm for her? Did he think that as a nurse she was accustomed to seeing naked male bodies and often indulged in casual sex? Say something, her mind screamed. When he didn't say anything, her mind urged her to explain, to tell him that she'd only been with one other man and that had been in an attempt to purge him from her thoughts. But she didn't say anything and her great, blue eyes locked on his face.

"What are you thinking?" he asked, and came to sit down beside her. He pulled the blanket up over her and tucked it behind her shoulders. Beneath it his fingers caught hers and crushed them in a tight grip. When she didn't answer, he asked, "Have you ever been in love?"

It was uncanny how he could sense her thoughts.

"I thought I was at one time."

"Did you feel with him what you felt with me?"

"No." It was the faintest of whispers. He was talking about her sexual experience, she was referring to her feeling for him three years ago.

He put his arm around her and pulled her close. "I'm glad," he said softly, proudly. Her head rested against his shoulder, and he leaned his cheek against her forehead. "Was he the only one?" She nodded, and he said again, "I'm glad."

It was very quiet, very peaceful. Beth stared into the fire and moved her palm across his chest to burrow into the space beneath his arm.

"No regrets?" His whisper accompanied light kisses and the brush of his mustache against her brow.

"What's this? Twenty questions?"

"No," he said after a long pause. "I just want to know all about you."

"I'm sorry." She turned her face into his neck. "I'm so confused."

"*Confused* confused? Or happy confused?"

"Both, I guess." She tilted her head to see his face. "We took a gigantic step in our relationship and—"

"Are you sorry?" The words were muffled against her lips.

"It was a beautiful sharing experience. I just don't

want you to think—" She halted in mid-sentence, not wanting to phrase her fear.

"You don't want me to think you're easy. Is that it?" Not waiting for an answer, he pressed his lips softly to hers. When he lifted his head, the corners of his mouth were raised in a half smile. "Honey, you're far from easy. That first night in Rochester I wanted to beg you to let me stay with you, but I knew you'd throw me out on my ear."

"You didn't even like me."

"Mmm . . . I played it cool, didn't I?" His eyes twinkled mischievously. "I thought you were an adorable kid when I came to be best man at the wedding, but when I came back and saw the woman you had grown to, I was determined you were going to come home with me. If you'd dragged your feet, I was going to get sick so you'd have to take care of me."

"Sick? That reminds me—I noticed that you're terribly warm. You may have a fever." She moved her fingers to the base of his throat and pressed the pulse beating there. Her own pulse raced so fast that she couldn't count his.

"Having you in my arms is enough to make my temperature rise." His fingers searched beneath the robe for her breast.

"Are you feeling all right?" Beth ran her hand over his heated flesh. Now that she thought of it, his skin had been warm when she came downstairs; hers had been a mass of cold goose pimples.

"Of course I feel all right, little Florence Nightingale. But if it will keep you fussing over me, I'll be happy to get sick." A hard rap on the kitchen door startled them. "There's Herb. Give me a kiss, love." Their lips met in tender, nipping, bittersweet kisses. The hard-knuckled rap sounded again, and Tom raised his head. "Thank you, darlin'." He got to his feet, bent to tuck the blanket snugly around her, and reached for the flashlight.

CHAPTER NINE

The wind stopped blowing when the sun came up. Beth pulled back the draperies that covered the large picture window and looked out over a winter wonderland. White snow, piled by the wind, lay in picturesque drifts several feet deep. Icicles, clear and sparkling in the sunlight, hung from the eaves of the house. Happiness danced in Beth's heart like a snowflake in the wind. I've got years of love saved up for you, Thomas, darling, she thought.

The man who was constantly in her thoughts had gone out to the utility buildings to check on the generator. As soon as he left the house, Beth had dashed upstairs to brush her teeth, have a quick wash, and dress in layers of warm clothing. Now she busied herself bringing all the houseplants into the kitchen so they would have the benefit of heat from the fireplace.

Then Sarah called.

"Is everything all right out there?"

"The electricity went off last night," Beth told her. "Thomas called the power company and they told him they had crews out looking for downed lines. In the meantime we have a fire in the fireplace and the generator is keeping the pipes from freezing." Beth couldn't suppress a giggle. "Thomas set a pan of water on the grate to boil. When he put the coffee in it, it boiled up and almost put out the fire."

"You sound happier this morning."

Oh, I am! My whole world has changed since last night, she thought. Aloud she said, "I guess I'm getting over the shock of the long trip."

"They're saying on the news that this is the most severe winter we've had in several years. All the major highways are closed and several deaths have been reported among stranded motorists. It'll take several days to dig out and get things back to normal." Her voice ended on a wistful note.

"Herb said this morning that just as soon as they have the essential chores done he'll start opening up the road to the highway. As it turned out, it's a good thing you didn't come home with us yesterday. The only warm place in the house is the kitchen. The rest of the rooms are cold as ice."

"My plants—"

"All safe. I brought them into the kitchen."

"Oh, Elizabeth, I'm so glad you'll be there when I come home!"

"So am I."

"Tell Thomas and Herb that I know how busy they

139

are at a time like this, and that there's no mad rush for them to come and get me. I'm just fine here, although I miss being home. And Beth . . . Thomas is really a sweet and gentle man."

For a long time after she hung up the phone Beth thought about what Sarah had said. *Thomas is really a gentle man.* What a strange thing to say. With a deep breath and a long sigh, she remembered how gentle, how considerate, how loving he had been.

It was almost noon when she heard the soft hum of the refrigerator and saw the light come on over the electric range. The power had been restored. Now, to make a really good cup of coffee and heat some canned soup. She'd have a hot meal ready when Herb and Thomas came back to the house.

It didn't take long for the house to warm up once the furnace fan was set in motion. Beth turned on the radio to hear the weather report. It was fifteen degrees below zero. It couldn't be *that* cold, she thought. It looks so beautiful out there in the white stillness.

When Beth heard a noise in the entry between the garage and the kitchen, she hurried to the door and flung it open. The smile of welcome on her face was quickly replaced by a puzzled frown when she saw Jerry Lewis, one of the men she and Thomas had picked up on the highway, standing before her. He stood silently grinning at her, with his hands in his pockets. She recognized the expression on his face immediately. *He was stoned!*

"What do you want?"

"Do I have to want somethin'?"

"Why are you here?" Beth kept her tone even.

"It's cold . . . out here," he said stupidly. His eyes were opened wide, the pupils mere pinpoints.

"I know it is. You'd better go back to the bunkhouse, where it's warm."

"Ain't no women out there."

Moving as naturally and as calmly as possible, Beth stepped out into the entry and picked up a coat that had fallen from the rack. When she turned back she found that he had moved around her and was going into the kitchen. She darted around in front of him.

"Hold it! I didn't invite you into the house."

"I know it." He spread his feet wide apart to steady himself.

"Please leave."

"Whaaat?"

"Leave. L-E-A-V-E. Go on back to the bunkhouse."

"I wanta stay here." He reached for her, and she stepped away.

"Your friend will be looking for you." Her voice had risen in pitch, and she reminded herself to stay calm.

"He ain't no friend. He's a bastard."

"Is that right? I really would appreciate it if you would leave, so I can get on with my work." Her heart began to beat in double time and her legs felt weak, but she knew she had to appear completely confident.

"I ain't goin' to bother. I'm just goin' to look at you."

"That's very flattering, but Mr. Clary will be angry if he comes and catches you here. He was kind enough to offer you shelter. The least you can do is respect his hospitality." Beth knew immediately that she shouldn't have used such strong words. His face tightened and his expression turned ugly.

"I don't care 'bout him! I could blow him away . . . just like that!" He snapped his fingers.

"I'm sure you could, but what would that prove?" Beth took a deep breath. She was beginning to feel frightened, and she searched her mind for every bit of information she'd learned on how to handle a situation such as this.

"It'd prove that I don't have to take nothin' from nobody," he replied belligerently.

"I see. Do you live in Cody?"

"Hell, no. I live in L.A."

"You're a long way from home. I'm sure you're not used to this cold weather."

"I ain't wantin' to talk 'bout no weather. I come to see a woman." He reached for her again, and Beth deftly sidestepped.

The outside door opened and Shiloh came bounding in, then slid to a halt when she saw the stranger in the kitchen. Behind her, Tom's tall form filled the doorway. Something in his expression brought back to Beth's mind the strange statement

Sarah had made earlier. *Thomas really is a gentle man.* He looked anything but gentle now. The intensity of his expression, laced with the dark scowl and beetled brows, was intimidating enough without the added leverage of the vicious oath that burst from his lips.

"What the hell are you doing in here?"

The man looked at him blankly, his head wobbling when he turned it. "What's it to ya, cowboy?" He grinned, seeming enormously pleased with himself.

Tom reached him in two steps. A heavy hand on his shoulder sent him spinning toward the door. "Did he touch you?" he bellowed at Beth as he moved.

Beth was shocked by the savagery of his tone. "No! He's stoned, Thomas. He's out of it. Don't you understand?"

"You're damn right I do. The low-life bastard! I've got no patience for dopers." He gave the man a vicious push. "Get the hell out of here!"

"Stop it! He's in no condition to go out there. He'll never find his way to the bunkhouse."

"Tough! That's his problem." With his hand clamped to the man's shoulder, Tom propelled him through the garage and shoved him out the door.

Beth grabbed her coat from the hook and followed. Jerry was picking himself up out of a snowbank where Tom had shoved him. He was still grinning when he got to his feet.

"Hey, what's goin' on?" Mike Cotter was running through the snowdrifts toward them.

"Get your stuff together. I'm taking you back to your car," Tom ordered, glaring at the man, his jaw muscles pulsing as he fought to contain his anger.

Beth waded through snow that reached halfway to her knees and put her hand on his arm. "How, Thomas? How can you take them? You'll never get through."

"Herb and I'll take them on the snowmobiles." He swore viciously. "The bastards have been shootin' drugs in the bunkhouse." He looked down at her as if just realizing she was there. "You don't have your boots on," he said impatiently, and swung her up into his arms. He carried her to the doorway. "Get back in there and dry your feet. I'll be back as soon as I get rid of them."

"Thomas . . ."

He didn't answer. He was the same as after he'd roughed up the cowboy in the restaurant. He seemed to retreat into himself. With apprehension gnawing at her, she watched him follow the two men across the snow-covered yard. Half an hour later she stood at the window and watched the two snowmobiles leave the ranch, headed toward the highway.

Twice she had seen Tom lash out with what she considered unnecessary force. All her life she had despised violence of any kind, and her sister was aware of that fact. Twice Sarah had made the remark that Thomas was a *gentle* man. Why would she say that? Was Thomas unable to control his temper? Was that why Sarah was trying to assure her that Thomas

144

didn't have a violent nature? She didn't want me to build up a dislike for him before I got to know him, Beth decided.

The afternoon passed slowly. After cooking a roast, banked with potatoes, carrots, and onions, Beth kept a vigil at the window and looked out into the early evening darkness, hoping to see lights coming up the lane. Doubts assailed her. It was still in the back of her mind that there was more between Sarah and Thomas than friendship. Was Sarah in love with him? How could she possibly not be in love with him? By six o'clock Beth's nerves were stretched almost to the breaking point.

When she finally saw the two beams of light approaching the house, she heaved a tremendous sigh of relief and tried to ignore the thudding in her chest. It was a strange but pleasant stirring within her, and she had a fleeting impression of how pioneer women had felt when their men returned from a dangerous mission.

She was taking the roast from the oven when she heard the familiar voice scolding the dog and telling her she would have to stay in the foyer until she was dry enough to come into the house.

"Hi." Thomas came through to the kitchen and leaned on the counter. Herb followed and closed the door.

"Are you hungry?" It seemed to Beth a sensible bit of chitchat while she was taking the roasting pan to the counter. Then she saw Thomas's drawn, tired, utterly weary face. The muscles in his jaw knotted as he clenched his teeth.

"I'd like some of that hot coffee, honey. I'm cold clear through to my bones." He pushed himself away from the counter, went to the fireplace, and stood with his arms folded on the mantel.

Beth darted a glance at Herb and saw that he was watching Tom with concern on his dark face. Her mind skittered in panic, and she went to join Tom where he stood with his head resting on his arms. Now she saw his broad shoulders shivering, and knew the reason for his clenched teeth. He was trying to keep them from chattering. She lay her hand on his arm.

"Are you sick, Thomas?"

"No, honey. Just tired and cold. It's been a hell of a day."

"Let me take your temperature. You have a fever. I'd like to know how high it is."

"Not now, sweetheart." The lines on each side of his mouth deepened. "I want to sit down for a while." The green eyes passed over her quickly. He sank down into a chair and leaned his head back wearily.

Beth took the Indian blanket from the back of the couch and draped it over him, tucking the ends behind him and down into the sides of the chair. She brushed the hair back from his face, then rested her hand lightly on his forehead. It felt hot and dry. She should have known this morning that he wasn't well! She continued to castigate herself while she put the

146

teakettle on to boil. She'd make a toddy if there was any whiskey in the house. Herb had gone down the hall to the bathroom. When he returned, Beth was waiting for him with the question.

"Is there any whiskey in the house?"

The big man moved easily. He reached into the cabinet above the refrigerator and brought out a bottle.

"A slug of this will warm him up quicker than anything."

"I was going to make a toddy, but perhaps you're right." She poured a small amount in a glass and took it to Tom. His eyes were closed. He looked so quiet and weary sitting there. Tenderness welled through her as she brushed a lock of hair back from his forehead. His eyes opened at the touch of her hand.

"Drink this and it'll warm you."

"I don't think I can, honey." He turned his face away from the smell. "My stomach isn't behaving very well."

Beth set the glass on the table. "Why don't you go up, take a hot bath, and go to bed? It could be that you've got a case of the good old-fashioned flu."

Tom's hand came out from under the blanket and searched for hers. She met it with a firm clasp. His eyes were bright with fever, and he squinted against the light from the lamp.

"My head feels like a thousand hammers are pounding on it," he said regretfully. "Tonight, of all nights, when I wanted to be with you, I feel like I've been hit by a semi."

"You didn't feel good this morning," she accused gently. "Why didn't you say something?"

"There was too much to do. I took a couple of aspirin and thought that would take care of it."

"Aspirin is not a cure-all. Come on, let's get you into bed."

Tom grinned in spite of his pain. "Just the words I've been wanting to hear."

Before she spoke, Beth glanced quickly to see if Herb had heard the remark. He was putting the food on the table.

"Are you sure you can't eat something?"

"Don't turn all nursey on me, love. I'm sorry I'm going to have to take myself away from you, but I feel like hell." He lurched to his feet and on unsteady legs made it to the stairs. Holding onto the railing, he climbed them and disappeared in the hallway above.

Beth stood looking after him, then moved to follow. Herb's voice stopped her.

"Give him a little time. No man wants his woman to see him throw up."

It was a while before the import of his words reached Beth's worried mind. When she turned to look at Herb, he was smiling gently.

"I'm not his— Did he say that?" Anger and embarrassment vied for dominance.

"No. But I saw the change in him this morning. It could only have been because of you."

Beth felt the warmth come up her neck to her face. "I suppose you think that—"

"I don't think anything. Everyone needs someone. Tom more than most."

Beth looked at him steadily. His dark eyes seemed challenging and vaguely envious. "How about you?"

"Me too." He waited a moment and said, "I'll go up and see if he's in bed. He has to be pretty sick before he'll give up."

"He may have Asian flu. He has the symptoms. If he isn't better by morning, I'll call and talk to his doctor. It may be that someone will have to bring out some medication."

"No problem. I can always get to town on the tractor, or someone can fly it out and drop it."

"That's a relief to know."

While Herb was upstairs, Beth put the roast back in the oven to keep warm. She was sure Herb would be hungry even if she and Tom were not. What a strange and gentle man the foreman was, with his quiet, dark face and soft voice. He was a man she could have fallen in love with if she hadn't met Thomas first.

Beth waited for what she considered a reasonable time before she went upstairs. She went to her room first and took stock of the medication in her first-aid kit. There wasn't anything there that could combat the infection causing Tom's fever. She had aspirin, of course, and a very mild form of penicillin tablet. Tom needed fluids, and probably the only thing he could keep in his stomach would be carbonated beverages. Thank goodness there were plenty of those on hand.

The door to Tom's room was ajar. Beth cautiously pushed it open and went inside. There were no lamps on, but in the light coming through the open door of the bathroom, she saw Tom on the bed and his discarded clothes on the floor beside it. Herb came out of the bathroom with a glass of water in his hand.

"He doesn't have anything left in his stomach, that's for sure."

"It'll be good if he can sleep." Beth stooped to pick up the clothes.

Herb set the glass on the table beside the bed. "He'll be all right while we eat supper. Sarah will be calling soon."

"She said she'd call around seven. It's almost that now."

"I won't tell her that Tom's sick. It'll just worry her. Time enough for that tomorrow."

Beth folded Tom's sweater and lay it on the bureau. "I'll let him sleep a couple of hours, and then I'll wake him and take his temperature."

Beth and Herb talked to Sarah when she called, and Herb smoothed over Tom's absence by saying he was upstairs at the moment. By the time the conversation was over, Beth was almost sure the foreman was in love with her sister. It was in the tone of his voice, his gentle encouraging words, and the softening of his harsh features when he talked to her. Now it remained to be seen if Sarah returned his affection or if it was Tom she had given her heart to.

"Did you have any more trouble with the men

when you took them to their car?" Beth inquired casually.

"Not much. We ran into a highway patrol officer and turned them over to him. It wasn't only pot they were using. They had some hard stuff too."

"Thomas has quite an explosive temper," she ventured shyly, and stole a glance at him.

He shrugged. "At least *he* tries to control it, which is more than I can say—" He broke off in mid-sentence and raised his coffee cup to his lips. Beth waited for him to say more, but when he spoke again, it was to tell her that this year they had driven the cattle into feeding pens and it was lucky they had because some of them would have died during the storm.

While Beth put the dinner things away, Herb went back up to check on Tom. "He's still sleeping," he told her when he returned. "I'm going to turn in. If you need me, punch number two on the dial. The phone will ring in the rooms above the garage."

"Thank you, I will. Good night, Herb."

Beth made sure the doors were locked and the lights off before she went up to her room to put on her granny gown, robe, and slippers. With the first-aid kit under her arm she went down the hall to Tom's room. The bedside lamp was on, and he watched her come into the room.

"How do you feel?"

"I'm freezing. Do you suppose you could find some extra covers?"

"There's a down comforter in my closet. Do you know where I can find the heating pad?"

"Sarah may have one in her room." He closed his eyes again.

Beth found the heating pad, plugged it in, and slipped it into the bed beneath his feet. She covered him with the extra comforter, moved a chair beside the bed and sat down.

"I'd take your temperature if I weren't afraid those chattering teeth would break it," she joked.

"I'll be okay in a little while. You could get in here with me and keep me warm. Jane Russell did it in an old movie I saw on TV."

She laughed softly. "I don't think you're quite as sick as you make out."

"I want to hold you. I want you to hold me." There was longing in his voice and his eyes pleaded with her.

Without hesitation she stood up and slipped out of her robe. His arm raised the covers and she had a glimpse of his naked chest before she lay down beside him and drew his head to her shoulder. With her free hand she tucked the covers firmly around him, then wrapped his chilled body with her arms and cradled him close. He snuggled his face into the curve of her neck with a sigh.

"You feel so good."

"Shh . . . go to sleep." Her lips moved over his forehead in soft, soothing kisses.

Gradually he relaxed and stopped shivering. Beth's

warm hand stroked the muscular thigh that lay across hers, trying to bring warmth to his chilled legs. She wasn't sure if what she was feeling for him was love for a man or the kind of love she would feel for a child. It was probably a mixture of both. All she knew was that she wanted to give to him whatever he needed.

Long after he was warm and sleeping, Beth lay with her thoughts going in several directions. Three years ago she had been sure that she loved this man, but with absence the love faded. Could it return with such terrific force that it was capable of consuming a person? They had satisfied each other's needs last night under the guise of pretended love. It had been his idea to use the word. Was she a substitute for her sister? The thought was so painful that her eyes flew open to stare at the ceiling. Tom stirred restlessly, and she raised her head so she could see his face. A new wave of feeling swept over her, one of tenderness. And she wondered if this man, of all men, was capable of making her life complete. Being too weary to try to answer the questions that plagued her, she gave herself up to the luxury of holding him, and finally she dozed.

The sound of Tom's voice woke her. She was so relaxed that at first she only thought she'd heard his slurred words. His body was hot and he had one bare arm out from under the covers. She covered him and tried to move a little away from him, but his arms closed around her and clamped her tightly to him.

"Damn you!" he muttered, and turned his face into her shoulder, rocking his head back and forth as if in torment. "Oh, Sarah! Goddammit! It's always been this way."

Beth was instantly alert. Her first thought was to wake him, because she didn't want to hear what he was saying, but then he began to talk again.

"Don't cry, Sarah. I'll take care of you." He groaned and flung out his arm. "You're pretty and sweet . . . don't worry. No one will ever know. It isn't wrong, Sarah . . . It isn't wrong to feel this way. . . ." His voice died away to incoherent murmurs and then silence.

A coldness settled around Beth's heart as if someone had plunged it into a freezer. Somewhere in her mind she had known all along that there was something more than a brother/sister relationship between Tom and her sister.

So many things fell into place now. Thomas moving Sarah up to his house, his concern for her, the urgency to bring her back from Minnesota to take care of her. His willingness to allow Sarah to decorate his house was a sure sign that he didn't intend to marry anyone else. Why was he keeping his feelings a secret? It had to be that he didn't want to hurt Herb, knowing that he, too, was in love with Sarah. No, that couldn't be. Men were seldom that considerate of other men's feelings where a woman was concerned. Maybe Sarah didn't return his love, and he had brought her here to make Sarah jealous—Beth's thoughts whirled in a riot of scornful accusations against both Thomas and her sister.

What are you going to do now, you fool? How could you have been so stupid? Tears slid slowly from the corners of her eyes and rolled down into her cheeks and into her hair. When Tom had recited the poetic words *I love you,* he had told her they were pretend, so how could she blame him now? How could he have known her words had come from her heart?

Easing her legs from their entrapment between his, she inched herself away from his long, hard body. Sleeping soundly, he didn't stir when she moved his limp arm aside and slipped out of the bed. She stood beside it for a long moment and looked down on his relaxed features. *You're a bastard,* she mouthed. A handsome, charming, cheating bastard, or you'd never have made love to me when you're in love with my sister.

The misery in her body grew, encompassing her heart and expanding into her soul. She hurried to her room before the volcano of tears erupted within her. At least some of her questions were answered.

CHAPTER TEN

Beth used the hours before dawn to condition herself for the new day. She counseled herself sternly. It wasn't as if she hadn't faced disappointment before. She had no one but herself to blame for not heeding the squirming little worm of doubt that had tried to wiggle into her reasoning. Almost lightheaded with the conflict in her brain, she bathed, dressed, and went downstairs. The heaven had lasted for only a few hours; surely the hell couldn't last forever.

Appropriately enough, the sun hid behind a bank of gray clouds. Gloom permeated the house and was suitable company for Beth's sagging spirits. Herb was in the kitchen. He poured her a cup of coffee while telling her he had looked in on Tom and found him still sleeping.

"I'll plow snow if nothing else comes up to claim my attention," he told her.

The rest of Beth's fading courage went out the door with Herb. She dreaded the moment she would face Thomas.

It happened sooner than she had expected. She looked up from the stove where she was cooking an egg, and there he was, leaning against the door frame. His hair was rumpled from sleep and there was the shadow of a night's growth of beard on his lean cheeks. He had slipped into a pair of faded jeans and a gray sweatshirt. Beth felt a fierce rush of resentment that he could stand there so calmly when her stomach felt as if a couple of cats were inside, clawing to get out.

"How do you feel this morning?" A calm voice and slight smile masked the wrenching ache that tore at her heart.

"Like I've been run over with a steamroller, and weak as a cat."

"I have a remedy for that. Sit down, I'll fix you some toast and eggs." She bent to take the egg poacher from under the counter, and when she straightened he was beside her. "Running around with bare feet is no way to get over the flu," she said coolly, and busily filled the pan with water.

Tom moved behind her and placed his hands on either side of her and braced himself against the counter. "When I went to sleep last night you were in bed with me. Why did you leave?" He pushed the hair away from her ear with his chin, and put his lips there. She shivered once, then hunched her shoulder to escape his touch.

"I'm busy, Thomas."

He pressed against her hips, imprisoning her against the cabinet while his tongue caressed her earlobe. Beth felt the unmistakable pressure of his masculine sex against her buttocks and tried to turn from it, but his hands had found their way up under her sweater and his palms flattened her breasts. Using more strength than was necessary, she dropped the pan in the sink and pushed him away from her.

"Stop it!"

Undaunted, he grinned at her lazily. "Are you a grouch this morning, sweetheart?"

"Yes, I am. I didn't get much sleep last night." Beth seized the excuse for her behavior.

"You didn't get much sleep the night before, either." A smile tugged at the corner of his mouth.

Sudden, hot anger rose in Beth. Cool it, she cautioned herself. If you lash out at him he'll know that what happened between you was more important to you than it was to him. Important? What a mundane word to describe it!

"You *are* feeling better this morning." She retrieved the pan from the sink and refilled it with water. I can't stand this, she groaned silently. Then, Yes, you can! Buck up, girl. Salvage your pride.

"I feel better. I must have had the twenty-four hour misery that makes the rounds once in a while. I'll take it easy today."

Beth walked around him to get to the stove. "Herb said to tell you he'll start plowing out the drive."

"Did he say anything about going in to get Sarah?"

"No," she said flatly. "How many eggs?"

"Two. Did Sarah call last night?"

"Yes. Herb talked to her. Toast?"

"Two, to start."

Beth was proud of the way she was handling herself. She had managed, with a great deal of effort, to remain calm during one of the most difficult situations she'd ever had to face. She refused to let her tears have their freedom and even contrived a small, cool smile when she set his breakfast before him.

"You said you didn't sleep well?" His voice had become taut, and when his hand shot out to close around her wrist, she felt the tension in his fingers and it added to her own.

"Only so-so," she muttered and lifted her shoulders in a careless gesture.

Tom's facial muscles tightened. "Are you feeling okay?"

"Sure," she said lightly, and moved to pick up her own plate. He was forced to release her arm.

"Then why in hell are you acting like a cow with her tit caught in the fence?"

Beth managed an indignant huff. "Just because you have the twenty-four hour misery, that's no excuse for being vulgar."

"Vulgar!" The sound that came from him was like a snort. Anger flickered in the eyes that raked her face before they became unfathomable.

"More toast?" she asked evenly.

His brows lifted and then fell. "No, thank you." His tone had turned decidedly cold.

Somehow, the morning passed. Beth was upstairs when Sarah called, so she was spared the pain of having to pretend that she was all bubbly with good feelings. She could hear Tom's voice, but couldn't and didn't want to hear what he was saying. Just for a moment she allowed herself to cry silently. Biting her lip, her eyes filled with tears before she hurried to the bathroom to dash them away with a spray of cold water. Oh, God! Am I going to be able to carry this off? she wondered.

When she went down to the kitchen to prepare lunch, Tom lay sprawled in the chair. He looked up when she came into the room. He still hadn't shaved and his face wore the look of a man with a lot on his mind.

"You're awfully quiet today," he observed.

"Am I?" Beth tried to smile and hoped her attempt at brightness would succeed. She went to the refrigerator and took out the cold roast in an effort to avoid a discussion. She was aware that Tom had come up behind her, and she moved before he could touch her.

"What's the matter with you? You act like a pup with its tail in a crack."

"First I'm a cow with my tit caught in the fence and now a pup with my tail in a crack. Flattering."

"I don't need any of your smart-ass answers," he snapped.

"I'm all right. See, I'm smiling." She spread her lips, showing all her teeth. "Will Herb be in for lunch?"

"I doubt it. Damn!" He struck the counter with the flat of his hand. Beth jerked her head around at the sound. She watched his features harden in a surge of anger.

"How do you feel about hot beef sandwiches for lunch?" Her voice was hoarse with the strain of attempting a normal tone. She leaned over the sink and ran water over her hands. As she reached for a towel, she heard the sound of a snowmobile close to the house. By the time she'd hung the towel back on the rack, the doorbell was ringing. Tom stalked to the door and flung it open with such force that the dog backed away and didn't dart into the kitchen as she usually did.

Beth greeted Pat O'Day with an overbright smile.

"Howdy, darlin'!" he said with a wink. "I see you haven't forgotten me."

"Of course not. Did you come out from town on your snowmobile?"

"Sure did. I came across country, as the crow flies. It's the only way to go." He stood grinning at her, his bright eyes openly admiring.

"You're in time for lunch." Beth glanced at a grim-faced Tom. "That is, if you can eat last night's leftovers."

"You betcha. I'm not fussy. I'll eat anything that don't bite me first." He glanced around at Tom. "Herb tells me you're under the weather, ol' hoss."

"Nothing to speak of," Tom said drily. "How's Herb doing? Has he got to the end of the lane?"

"Yeah. He's out to the gravel road. The county man is coming up from the other end. They should have the road open anytime now." Pat turned his attention back to Beth. "What can I do? I can't stand to see a pretty woman workin' all by herself."

Beth smiled at him. It was almost impossible not to. "I'll be glad for your help. Cooking isn't my long suit." She avoided looking at Thomas. "But you must wash your hands first. Cook's rule number one."

"May I interrupt long enough to excuse myself?" Tom stood, adamantly fingering the stubble on his chin.

"Go ahead, ol' man. Don't let me keep you from anythin'," Pat said cheerfully. "You don't have to entertain me. Just watchin' this pretty thin' is all the entertainment I need."

Tom gave a derisive snort. Beth met his eyes briefly, but long enough to see the disapproval reflected there. Then with characteristic arrogance he stalked from the room, leaving her seething with impotent rage.

During lunch Beth had the uncanny sensation of sitting on the edge of a volcano about to erupt. Tom had come to the table with a freshly shaved face and wearing an open-necked knit pullover shirt. Beth refused to acknowledge that the flutter in her heart was caused by the familiar scent of his after-shave when he passed behind her chair. She was immensely relieved that it wasn't necessary for her to hold up an end of the conversation. The men discussed the storm, cattle feeding, and the underground cable business, leaving her free to concentrate on getting the fork from her plate to her mouth and the food down her throat without choking on it.

Surely it will become easier, she told herself. This is the first day. Tomorrow will be better, the day after that better still. That was the way it had worked before, so why not this time? I've only got to get through this day, she reasoned. Tomorrow Sarah will be home.

Beth was thankful for Pat's company. After she loaded the dishwasher she found him bent over a huge jigsaw puzzle laid out on a card table in the living room. She wasn't a puzzle fan and hadn't tried to put any of the pieces in place, realizing it was Sarah's project because of the raised chair beside the table.

"Sit down and give me a hand," Pat urged. "I'm a puzzle freak from way back. Can't resist 'em."

A couple of hours passed almost pleasantly. Finally Pat's interest in the difficult puzzle began to wane. "Would you like a ride on my machine before I head back to town?" When he stood beside Beth, their eyes were on a level. His eyes were blue and merry, hers blue and desperately trying not to mirror the misery she was feeling.

"I'd love to go. How cold is it?"

"Not as cold as yesterday. Only nine below, but no wind to speak of."

"Super. Give me a few minutes to get on my long johns."

"I'll be glad to help," Pat called after her as she started up the stairs.

Beth turned to smile at him and saw that Tom had come in from the family room and was watching her from the doorway. The light retort died on her lips and she continued on, hurrying to get out from under the critical, angry blaze of his intense green eyes. She couldn't help shivering at the thought that very soon she would have to account for her actions.

Pat started the snowmobile and Beth slipped into the seat behind him. The snow was light and the churning lugs of the machine left a soft, white cloud behind them. Beth's spirits rose as they headed for open country. The breeze rushing against her face and the snow whipping around her cleared her head and soothed her taut nerves.

Pat was a pleasant companion who laughed easily. His wolfish, flirtatious ways were a come-on that was not meant to be taken seriously. Beth was comfortable with him.

At the top of a hill he stopped the machine and grinned over his shoulder at her. "Your cheeks look like two red apples."

"Crab or Delicious?"

"De-licious. Definitely Delicious."

"You've got a line a mile long, Patrick O'Day."

"Nicest thing anyone's said to me all day." He got off the machine so she could turn around. "Look at that view. Pretty, isn't it."

Beth followed his gaze. Spread before them was a panorama of ranch buildings surrounded by tightly branched pine trees. Her eyes dwelled on Tom's house for a long moment and then on the three smaller houses behind and to the left of it. She wondered which one of them Sarah and Steven had lived in. Farther to the west she could see the feeding pens and the utility buildings, but her eyes kept coming back to the long brown house with smoke curling from its chimney.

"It looks like a scene on a Christmas card," she remarked.

"Yeah, it does," Pat said seriously, and then

laughed as if he disliked having to say something serious. "I'd better get you back. I don't think ol' Thomas was too pleased that you came out with me. He looked like he was about to blow a fuse."

"He's had the flu. I don't think he feels well today." Beth smiled carefully. "A nurse gets used to grouchy patients and pays them no mind."

It seemed to take less time to get back to the house than it did to reach the hill. Almost before Beth was aware of it, Pat eased the machine up to the garage door and turned off the motor.

"Thanks. I enjoyed that."

"My pleasure. We'll do it again." A drift of snow hanging on the eave of the roof let go just at that moment and cascaded down on Pat, showering him with the white stuff. He looked at Beth accusingly.

"I didn't do it," she said. "It wasn't my fault." She began to back away. He stalked her and she turned to run. "I didn't do it!" she shrieked between peels of laughter. When she saw that he was going to catch her, she grabbed up a handful of snow and threw it at him. The snowball connected just as he reached for her and they went tumbling into the snow.

"I'll teach you to laugh at me!" Pat sat astride her and calmly washed her face with a handful of snow.

When he let her go, he ran to the snowmobile and Beth sat up, sputtering. "I'll get you for that, you . . . jerk!" she yelled.

He laughed uproariously, put the machine in gear, and roared away.

Beth sat in the snow for a moment before she rolled to her knees and stood. She glanced at the house and saw Tom standing in the window. Immediately tension returned, winding around her until she thought her taut nerves would snap. Not wanting to face him just now, she walked around to the back of the house, toward the bunkhouse, tack house, machine sheds, and barns. She passed them and walked on toward the three small houses, each set in its own landscaped yard. The houses were small compared to the big house. They looked to be two-bedroom cottages.

As she walked along, a glimmer of an idea struck her. Tom had said that there was no one living in one of the houses. She wondered if he would allow her to live there. Sarah didn't need a live-in nurse, and by living out here she would be able to avoid Tom and still be available to care for her sister. How could Tom refuse the request?

Feeling better now that there was in sight, at least, one solution to her dilemma, she trudged head down back to the house.

Only Shiloh met her at the door. One quick look told her she might be able to make it to her bedroom without running into Tom. Without haste, in case he came out of one of the rooms and was watching her, she went up to the room that had been assigned to her. Once inside she took a deep breath and lay down on her stomach across the bed.

Beth hadn't intended to sleep, but she did. She woke to near darkness and sat up on the side of the bed. Five o'clock. She hadn't given a thought to fixing an evening meal. Then a wave of uncharacteristic resentment rose in her. She hadn't come out here to be a cook! Let them fix their own damn dinner! She'd take a bath.

A couple of hours later she felt as if she couldn't stay in the bedroom another minute. Not for anything did she want Tom to think she was avoiding him. It would put too much emphasis on what had happened between them. She glanced at herself in the mirror and was satisfied with the way she looked. The velour pants and top showed off her willowy figure to its best advantage, and the blue did wonderful things to her dark hair and blue eyes. Not that she was dressing to impress Thomas Clary, she hastily told her image in the mirror. She needed to know that she looked reasonably attractive, needed it to support her sagging self-confidence.

Tom was standing at the kitchen range. He glanced up and the look on his face knocked her heart backward a beat. The look was there for only a few seconds, but there was no mistaking it. He looked like a kid who had got up on Christmas morning and found his stocking empty.

"Need some help?"

"No, thanks." He glanced at the clock above the kitchen sink. "Herb will be in soon."

She hadn't expected this quiet indifference. She glanced at his profile. He was staring down into a skillet, stirring vigorously, ignoring her. The phone rang and for an instant Beth was startled. Her eyes were still on him when he looked up.

"Get that, will you?"

Beth picked up the phone. It was Pat.

"I just wanted to let you know that I made it back to the big metropolis."

"I wasn't worried about you, Pat, but it's nice of you to call and report in."

"I almost wish I hadn't called, if that's the attitude you're going to take. Didn't you worry even a little bit?"

"Well, maybe a little." Through the screening veil of her lashes Beth studied Tom's face. He was still stirring cream gravy in the skillet, although he had turned off the burner.

"Are you coming into town tomorrow?" Pat asked.

"I plan to come in and consult with Sarah's doctor. She's coming home tomorrow."

"Will you have time to have lunch with me?"

"I'll ask Thomas." Beth put her hand over the phone. "Will we have time to have lunch in town tomorrow?"

He shrugged. "It's up to you," he said indifferently. "But Jean and Sarah will be anxious to get home."

Piqued by his nonchalance, Beth was tempted to accept Pat's invitation, but out of consideration for Sarah, she said, "We won't have time, Pat. But thanks just the same."

"Okay, sweet thing. Another time."

"Bye, Pat." Beth hung up the phone.

"Sorry to throw a monkey wrench in your little tête-à-tête." The words were half muffled.

Beth was tempted to tell him to speak up if he had anything to say, but the phone rang again. She lifted the receiver without being told to.

"Hello?"

"Elizabeth!" Sarah's excited voice broke into her thoughts. "I can hardly believe I'll be there with you this time tomorrow night. I swear the last few days have been the longest of my life."

"Mine too. Have you made an appointment for me to talk to your doctor?"

"In the morning at nine. Can you make it here by then?"

"I'm sure we can, but wait. I'll ask Thomas."

Sarah laughed. "He'll be here, or Herb will. What's he doing, anyway?"

"Here he is, you can find out for yourself." Beth held out the phone. His eyes held hers for a long moment before he reached for it.

"Hi, Sarah."

Tom's eyes made a continuous, searching study of Beth's face while he talked. In the oppressive tension between them, she suddenly had trouble breathing; her lungs hurt with the effort. Jarred into action, she went past him to the table and rearranged the silver he had placed beside the dinnerwear.

"We've missed you, too, honey." The tender tone of Tom's voice spoke a thousand silent words and

169

caused excruciating pain to Beth's already wounded heart. "No, Herb hasn't heard if Susan will come for Christmas. He'll probably pick you up tomorrow. You can ask him then." Beth took a deep breath during the silence that followed. "Do you want to talk to your sister again? Wait, I think Herb's coming in. You can ask him about Susan."

In a few moments Herb stood in his stocking feet, his face and hands red from the cold, and talked to Sarah in a low, patient voice. For just the tiniest second Beth felt a stab of envy. Her beautiful sister had all the love and respect a woman could want from two very special men.

Tom seemed preoccupied during the meal. He spoke only when Herb asked him a question, ate sparingly, and left the table to watch the evening news while Beth and Herb lingered over coffee. While Beth was arranging the dishes in the dishwasher, it occurred to her that the quiet foreman was aware of the undercurrent of tension between her and Thomas and had made an effort to ease things for her.

The bedroom was her sanctuary.

Beth glanced at the clock. It was only eight o'clock. Thank God she had brought a supply of paperbacks with her. She admitted, now that she was in the safety of the bedroom, that it was rude of her to come upstairs without a word to Thomas or Herb. But, dammit, she wasn't ready for a confrontation with Thomas, and it was bound to happen if she was left alone with him. With a painfully aching heart she prepared for bed.

It was ten o'clock. For the last couple of hours Beth had been trying to get interested in first one novel and then another. She lay propped on the pillows, her feet tucked in the bottom of her granny gown. In exasperation she tossed the novel to the bedside table. The story had all the right ingredients: handsome, virile hero; feminine, but strong-willed heroine; an exotic setting. Yet nothing was happening in the story that could compare with what was going on in her own life. She pulled the covers up under her chin and sank down into the bed.

The door to the hall was just beyond the end of the bed. Beth was looking at it, her mind on how she was going to approach Thomas about moving into the tenant house, when it opened slowly, and Thomas was standing there. It happened so smoothly that she blinked, unsure whether the figure lounging against the door frame was real or imaginary.

"Is something . . . wrong?" she stammered.

"You know damn good and well there is."

"What is it? What's happened?"

"You know *what's happened*. Cut the dumb Dora act." He came to the side of the bed.

"We can discuss whatever is on your mind in the morning," she said coolly. She didn't like the disadvantage of lying in bed and having to look up at him.

"We'll talk about it now." His glance moved from the bedclothes to her face.

"Say what you've got to say. I've a few things to say myself." Better to attack than be attacked, she thought bitterly.

"I'm listening."

"I'd like to move into your tenant house and live there while I'm here with Sarah."

"You think you'll need more privacy to entertain O'Day? Is that it?"

"Sarah won't need a live-in nurse," she said, ignoring the barb. "She and I can still spend a lot of time together, and I can give her the moral support and the medication from there as easily as from here."

"Pat just separated from his wife. Did he tell you that?"

Again she ignored his words. "I have savings. I can pay rent and utilities. It isn't as if it would cost you anything to allow me to live there."

"Shut up!" he roared. "Shut up about the damned house! You've got your tail over the line and I want to know why."

"I don't know what you're talking about."

"The hell you don't!"

"If you're referring to— If you think that because we had a romantic interlude it's going to be a permanent affair, then you're painfully mistaken."

Tom's hands reached for her. She was sure he was going to shake her. Volatile anger simmered beneath every move he made and every breath he drew. It took all her willpower not to cringe from his wrath.

"How could I have been so wrong about you?" Soft words came through his face of stone.

"How could I have been so wrong about you?" She threw the words back at him. "You lay down the rules!" She was shouting now. "You said pretend! Do you think that every woman you take to bed is in love with you?" Tears spurted. Angry tears. Dammit to hell! Why did she have to cry every time she got angry? Ashamed of her tears, she lashed out at him to hide her shame. "So we had a one night frolic. It didn't mean any more to me than it did to you. We're living in the twentieth century, for God's sake! It happens all the time, even between people who don't know each other. Haven't you heard of the swingers who swap wives? Just because you love one person doesn't necessarily mean you can't enjoy sex with another. Right?" Only later did Beth ask herself how such utter nonsense could have spewed from her mouth.

"Wrong!" Tom gripped her shoulders and lifted her upright in bed. "I could slap you!" he gritted.

The violence of his gaze locked with the anger of hers. She sensed the power struggle within him as he fought to bring his rage under control.

"Damn you!" she shouted. She lifted her hand to hit him. He flung her down on the pillows. "You're a bastard," she hissed. She was too angry to care what he did to her.

"What are you?" He rammed his hand into his pocket, brought out a fistful of bills, and flung them on the nightstand. "Your pay for the other night, and tonight!"

"No!"

"Yes!" He fell across her, pinning her to the bed. His strong fingers curled into the tender flesh of her upper arms.

"No!" She struggled wildly, hating him as much as she loved him, twisting and kicking, her movements hampered by the weight of the bedcovers. Rolling her head from side to side, she tried to evade his lips, but his mouth came down to ravage hers, plundering its softness and smothering her frantic cries of protest.

There was no escape. She was held so tightly that she could feel every bone in his body even through the bedclothes. The brutal kiss seemed to go on and on, and Beth wondered vaguely if this helplessness was what a woman felt when she was being attacked by a stranger. Blackness swam on the fringes of her consciousness as the strength was drained from her.

When she stopped struggling, Tom lifted his lips from her mouth and moved them to her temple. His hand moved up from her shoulder to slide beneath her head and hold it firmly in his grasp. Beth was trembling, drinking in air while her bruised lips throbbed. She could taste the blood on her tongue where he had ground her lips against her teeth. Tears spilled from her eyes. She was so steeped in misery that at first she didn't realize his lips were caressing away the wet rivulets that streamed down her face.

His lips returned to hers and she flinched from the pressure of his mouth on her cut lips. He raised his head. Beth's eyes were tightly closed, but she knew he was looking at her.

"Oh, God! Oh, sweetheart . . . What have I done?" His husky voice broke. Beth could feel the uneven motion of his chest against her breasts, and she squeezed her eyes tightly to hold back the tears. "I'm sorry! Sweet . . . sweet . . . I'm sorry. . . ."

Gently his lips stole over her face and gradually moved to hers, pried her lips apart and began sensually to lick away the hurt. His tongue sought to heal the cut, his lips caressed, and his mustache, soft and sweetly familiar, brushed her cheek.

His tenderness offered her a release from her own frustrations, and she returned his kisses eagerly. Just for a while nothing mattered as long as he touched her, held her, and made love to her.

CHAPTER ELEVEN

"I'm sorry! I'm sorry I hurt you, darlin'." Tom's lips traveled over her face, blotting her tears. He placed the softest of kisses on her bruised, swollen lips. "Are you okay now?"

"Yes." Beth knew she would have fought to the last breath if he had attempted to overpower her physically, but she was vulnerable to his attack of seduction. What he couldn't obtain with sheer force he could easily get with a sensual caress.

"I'm sorry." He kept repeating the words. "I'll never hurt you again. I never want to see that look of terror on your face." A groan came up from deep in his throat and he nuzzled his face into the side of her neck as if writhing in pain.

Sensations buffeted Beth in waves. The vulnerability of this man, the pleasure of his hands tracing the contours of her body, the stimulating caress of his mouth against her neck, all combined to lull her into a sensuous limbo. She was lost.

Tom lifted his head, letting the heat of his breath fan her lips. "Am I forgiven?" he murmured thickly.

"Yes," she whispered in the frustration of guilt over loving him.

Seconds later she was swept away by his deep, passionate kisses, until she didn't care anymore. Drugged with erotic sensations, Beth was only slightly aware when he moved away from her to throw back the covers so he could stretch out beside her and curl his arms and legs around her. With gentle pressure he fitted her body to his. His hand cupped her rounded bottom, his arm held her breasts crushed to his chest. She could feel his throbbing hardness and his warmth through her nightgown. He seemed content merely to hold her, and Beth fought to block out everything but this moment, this night.

"What are you thinking?" He placed sweet, chaste kisses on her mouth.

"I'm . . . pretending. . . ." The words were wrenched from her. Her hand crept up over his shoulder and her fingers moved in his hair, pulling his lips to her waiting mouth.

He drew in a long, shaky breath and stroked the hair back from her temples, his fingers caressing her cheek.

"What do you really feel for me?" he asked wearily.

She moved her hand to his chest and felt his heart thudding beneath it. The rest of him was still, with a peculiar, silent waiting. She moved restlessly against him.

"Why bring that up now? Don't you want to love me? Can't you pretend one more time?" she whispered.

"I want to love you now, tomorrow, forever. . . ." The hand on her buttocks pulled her against the surge of his groin and held her there. "But I want more than to have sex with you."

"Can't you pretend, if I can?" Her voice rose with her disappointment. She tried to push him away with her hand on his chest. She needed time to think. Something hurt inside her, and she swallowed hard.

"If that's what you want." The muttered words, barely coherent, were thickly whispered in her ear. "I'm no saint! I'll take you this way if it's all I can have." He began to stroke her, whispering words of seduction as he teased the corner of her mouth with his. "Beautiful . . . sweet . . ." His hands slid under her gown and lifted it to whisk it away. "Perfect. Your body is perfect . . . beautiful . . . heaven . . ." He muttered reverently, and kissed the rosy peak of her breast.

He left her to sit on the side of the bed. In the few seconds it took him to take off his clothes, Beth fought a battle with her pride. *No,* it screamed! He's using you to satisfy his sexual lust. What about my sexual lust? her nerves screamed back. I want him to make love to me one more time.

Her arms were open and welcomed him when he turned. The deeply buried heat in her body seemed to flare out of control. She sought his mouth hungrily and moved her hands over his sides and back, digging into the smooth muscles, loving the feel of his flesh. She felt the powerful tug of desire for him and admitted what her subconscious mind had known since the moment he entered the room. She wanted him and was glad he had come to her.

"Thomas, Thomas—" She was hungry for him and returned his caresses with all the instinctive sexuality of her young body.

"Shh . . . darlin'. Be still and let me love you." He kissed her soft rounded breasts, nibbled with his teeth, nuzzled with his lips. He was deliberately slow, giving her pleasure and at the same time pleasing himself. His lips moved to her mouth, exploring its shape and the texture of her lips and tongue until she was gasping for breath. He whispered endearments during the brief intervals when he was not taking the lips she offered so eagerly. "Sweet, sweet, darlin' girl . . ."

His hands moved over her, touching her from breast to thigh. She tangled her fingers in his hair and the strands fell across her breasts in an exquisite caress. He made small biting tracks across her shoulders and down the sides of her breast, then nibbled his way across her stomach, causing her to suck it in as wild desire swept through her. His fingers replaced his lips and traveled lower, as if compelled to know every inch of her.

Beth had never felt anything like the sensual enjoyment his seeking fingers were giving her. She knew the excruciating drive to be satisfied and to satisfy him. Her hand moved between them and enclosed the hard muscle that leaped and thrust in primitive desire.

Tom's muscular body slid over hers. It was hard, warm, and satin smooth. The velvety touch of him, hard and throbbing, nudging, seeking to fill her, started a fire that surged through the seat of her femininity, causing involuntary shudders of delight. He continued to speak to her in snatches of tender, soothing words.

"Is this what you want, my sweet love?" His fingers stroked; the tumult in her body grew. "Be mine and let me be yours," he murmured. "I'll take away that sweet ache. Be still, love. Soft is best—trust me." He entered her slowly. There were no sharp or hard thrusts. He lay still and she could feel his great body tremble with the effort it took to hold back. "Ah . . ." he sighed. He lifted his face to look at her.

His green eyes were dark with feeling and burned into hers.

Beth had the strange sensation of not knowing where his body ended and hers began. She could feel the pressure deep inside her as he gradually tilted her hips while his eyes held hers. She knew at that moment she would be forever his.

"Slowly, sweetheart," he murmured as she began to move. His mouth came over her mouth, his breath and hers one. He caressed her lips with his, his tongue making little jabbing forays along the inside of her mouth. Ever so slowly he penetrated her deeper with a slow, sensuous motion.

Beth clutched him tightly and ran her hands over the warm skin of his back. Heat radiated from his body to hers, sending her into a rapture of love so exquisite it made her head spin with desire. A small sound came from her lips, and rippling tremors ran through her inner being. Her arousal intensified to so great a pitch that she thought she would cry out. Fire ran along her nerves and her eyes flew open to look directly into two bottomless green pools.

"Talk to me. Tell me what you feel."

"Oh, darling . . . I feel you everywhere!"

"Look at me. We'll soar together." He said the words slowly, carefully.

"Yes, yes . . ." Beth gazed into eyes luminous with desire, knowing that nothing would ever compare to this moment.

The strokes came with a driving, primitive rhythm;

mutual strokes of belonging and possession. *Soar! Soar!* The word ricocheted through her mind as they climbed together to the cloudlike formation that cradled them. Beth's open eyes were unseeing as the world exploded and sent her spinning into warm, misty darkness. The only solid things in the universe were the arms around her, the lips that moved to cover hers, and the pulsing hardness inside her that she held cradled in the loving folds of her body. Beth felt as if her soul were reeling somewhere above her as Tom's passion erupted and filled her to the core.

They settled to earth once again. He lay with his face nestled in her tumbled hair, breathing deeply. When he finally stirred, it was to ease himself up on his elbows. He looked solemnly into wide blue eyes and reverently kissed her eyelids, one after the other, smoothing the damp hair back from her face with gentle fingers.

"Don't say anything," he murmured, and rolled onto his side, taking her with him. He reached for the covers and tucked them around them, groped for the light switch, and the room was plunged into darkness.

Beth lay tightly against his body, her head resting on his shoulder. A sigh trembled through her, and she closed her eyes. She had to sort out her emotions, untangle the confusion that had brought her to this state. She needed this time to think, but she couldn't remember a time when she was so weary in body, weary in soul, confused in mind. She stifled a groan as her mind began summoning back, in feverish detail, the words Thomas had murmured in his fever about Sarah.

The tears that trickled from her eyes rolled down her cheeks and onto his shoulder. He slowly stroked her back in silent communication. He didn't speak, and she was glad. How could she tell him she was sick with self-disgust, sick with guilt for wanting him, sick because she knew what he felt for her was only lust.

His hand touched her gently, as though she were fragile and infinitely precious. "Are you warm?" He tucked the blanket close behind her.

"Uh-huh."

"Go to sleep." Low, husky whispers came to her ears. "Things will work out. Trust me. Things have happened too fast for you. Time will take care of it." His lips pressed tiny kisses on her forehead, his voice a shivering whisper. "This is only the beginning for us."

"No," she groaned, but the thought of never having this pleasure again was a stab of agony in her heart. "There's more to life than this."

"Give us time and we'll have it, darlin'," the seductive voice whispered in her ear. "Shh . . . sleep."

The completeness of their lovemaking had left Beth exhausted. She fell asleep almost immediately, falling into a deep, satisfying slumber. But all night long she was subconsciously aware of the warm, male body pressed to her own, the heavy weight of the arm across her body, and the hand that cupped her breast.

"Elizabeth." Her name was a soft whisper wooing her from the depths of sleep. "Wake up, Beth." The voice was a little louder, more urgent. "C'mon, sleepyhead. Wake up."

Reluctantly she opened her eyes and pushed her hair back from her face. Thomas was standing beside the bed.

"What time is it?"

"Time for you to get up if you're going to town with Herb. He'll leave in about thirty minutes." He squatted on his heels beside the bed. "You were sleeping so soundly when I got up, I didn't have the heart to wake you, although I wanted to." His eyes glittered, and his mustache tilted when he grinned. Beth rolled her face into the pillow. More than anything in the world she wanted to reach out and put her arms around his neck. "I brought you a cup of coffee. Don't you think that deserves a morning kiss?"

"Sure." She made a kissing sound with her puckered lips and reached for the mug on the table.

"Won't do." Thomas captured her reaching hand with his, leaned over her, his mouth just touching hers. "Good morning," he whispered against her lips, then increased the pressure of his moist kiss. His lips moved with incredible gentleness over her mouth. It was a giving kiss, tender, and if she didn't know better, loving. It was almost more than she could bear without bursting into tears.

He sat back on his heels and looked at her. "I've got work to do this morning, but I'll try to be here when you get back. I thought we'd have a celebration tonight to welcome Sarah home. We'll have everyone in for steaks. How does that sit with you?"

"Fine." She didn't know what else to say. Besides, she thought, why should he be asking her?

"Okay. I've got to get going." He leaned toward her and covered her lips with his. "See you later." His voice was a whisper when they finally broke the kiss. He went to the door, turned with a happy smile on his face, and winked at her.

Beth sat up in bed and reached for the coffee. She didn't understand him at all. What's more, she didn't understand herself. No wonder he was smiling, she thought angrily. The woman he loves and a mistress both under one roof; what more could he ask for?

She was still thinking the same thoughts while sitting in the station wagon beside Herb. She had very carefully gone over every word Thomas had spoken last night, and he hadn't said a word about love or a lasting relationship. All she meant to him was a warm body in bed.

"The highway is completely cleared in spots." Herb's voice cut into her thoughts. "There'll be a lot more snow in town, but they've got good equipment and a good crew. They'll have most of it hauled away by now."

"How long have you worked at the ranch?"

"About ten years, off and on."

"Then you knew Steven, Sarah's husband."

"Yeah."

Beth waited for him to say more. When he didn't, she said, "My parents and I met him when Sarah brought him home to be married. He looked an awfully lot like Thomas, though not as big."

"That's where the resemblance ended. They were nothing alike." His voice was suddenly curt, and he changed the subject to remark about the new wing being added to the hospital. "It'll be there on the west side." He parked the car in a snow-packed parking lot. "When we get ready to go, you and Sarah can meet me at the emergency entrance so she won't have to walk on this snow."

The long gleaming corridors, the rattle of carts full of dishes, and the familiar smell of medication brought a quiver of homesickness to Beth. This had been her world for a long time. She had moved in it with an awareness of all that went on, but now she was here as a visitor, and she accepted the cheerful smile given by the nurse on duty.

"Hello, Herb. Mrs. Clary is waiting for you. Are you Mrs. Clary's sister? I thought so," she said when Beth nodded. "Dr. Morrison will see you. Come this way."

Beth liked the doctor immediately. He was young, balding, and very professional. He was also very interested in Sarah's case. Beth was able to spot that at once. She could tell that he was impressed when she stated her qualifications and was able to converse

185

with him about her sister's condition. When she left his office twenty minutes later, it was with his neatly typed instructions in her purse and his assurance the medication and the equipment she needed to give the shots would be waiting at the reception desk.

The door to Sarah's room was open when Beth reached it. Dressed in warm slacks and a heavy sweater, her blond hair combed in swirls around her carefully made-up face, her eyes bright, Sarah looked young and happy.

"Elizabeth! I'm so excited about going home. Herb said he's going to sit on me if I don't calm down."

"How are you?" Beth embraced her sister.

"Fine. Just fine now that I'm going home." Sarah turned and held out her hand to the woman beside her. "Beth, this is Jean, one of my dearest friends."

Only one word could describe Jean: plain. She was a heavyset woman with flyaway gray hair and small eyeglasses perched on her nose. When she smiled, she showed more gums than teeth, and it was evident she smiled easily. Beth took the hand she offered.

"No matter what, she'll say she's fine," Jean said, still smiling.

"I'm glad you were able to be with her," Beth murmured.

"It wasn't no chore a'tall, let me tell you. Sarah and me can always find something to talk about."

"I'll take the cases down to the car," Herb said, and picked them up.

"Did you bring the things I asked for?" Sarah asked quickly.

"Sure did." He set the bags down, reached into his pocket, and handed her a couple of small packages carefully wrapped in white tissue paper. "I picked out the ones I thought you liked best."

"Little gifts for my nurses," Sarah explained. "Herb and I made these stained-glass leaded ornaments." She unwrapped one and held it up by the string attached to the top. It was a beautiful little owl with brown wings, a blue body, and large amber eyes.

"You *made* this? It's beautiful!" Beth exclaimed.

"Herb and I together." Sarah's eyes flashed to the tall silent man standing beside the door. "Herb's very artistic."

Herb gave a snort of disgust—Beth was sure to hide his embarrassment—and picked up the cases. "I'll bring the car up to the door."

Sarah said her good-byes. It was obvious that she was a favorite patient. Nurses were still waving and smiling when the elevator door closed and they descended to the lower level.

With Sarah tucked into the front seat of the station wagon, Beth and Jean in the back, they headed back to the ranch. Sarah and Jean exclaimed over the amount of snow that had piled up during the storm and asked questions about what had happened at home since they had been away. Beth mentioned the two stranded motorists they had picked up, and Sarah picked the details out of the usually quiet foreman. Beth thought he talked more on the ride from town than he had during the whole time she had known him, and she wondered if Sarah was aware that the man was in love with her. What were Sarah's feelings? As far as she could tell, she didn't treat him any differently from the way she treated Thomas.

When they reached the ranch yard, Herb drove down to the tenant house and let Jean out, then back to the house and pulled into the garage.

"Oh, look! Shiloh is waiting for me." Sarah opened the car door.

"Watch that hound," Herb growled. "She'll get you all wet."

"Are you glad to see me, girl? I'm glad to see you too." Sarah patted the shaggy head, and the dog wagged her tail so hard it swung her body from side to side. Sarah's happy laughter rang out and Beth caught a glimmer of a smile on Herb's face.

In the house Sarah went from room to room, looking at her plants. "They came through just fine, Beth," she called. "You didn't finish the puzzle, Herb."

"I was waiting for you," he said quietly, and continued on up the stairs with her bag.

Suddenly Beth was almost as sorry for him as she was for herself. "Would you like some lunch?" she asked when he returned. "I could scare up a sandwich and soup."

"Thanks. Then I've got to get crackin'."

"Are you going down to the south pens, Herb?" Sarah asked. "Thomas said he wouldn't be in until the middle of the afternoon."

Beth's hands trembled as she opened the soup. Thomas must have called Sarah before he left this morning.

"He drove the semi down. I'll go in the pickup and bring him back." Herb settled himself on a kitchen stool. "Now don't you two be doin' anything about the bash we're having tonight. Tom laid out steaks to thaw, Jean said she'd throw something together, and we'll microwave potatoes. After that, everyone's on their own."

"How many will be here?" Beth was trying terribly hard not to feel left out of the plans.

"Probably about twelve," Sarah said, then to Herb, "Is everyone coming?"

"As far as I know."

"Twelve?" Beth said in a worried tone.

"Don't worry. We've had as many as twenty here for supper on the spur of the moment, and my two men handled everything perfectly."

My two men. Beth slumped against the counter and kept her face turned away from the two, who continued to chat about the celebration they planned. All her life Beth had been a fighter, fighting for what she wanted, what she considered right. One time in her life she had been forced to retreat, and that was when Thomas made no attempt to get in touch with her when he came back to Wyoming after the wedding, after she had fallen so desperately in love with him and her pride had refused to allow her to get in touch with him. The hurt had not lasted nearly as long as she had expected it to. Would it be the same this time? she wondered.

She'd better begin to set the wheels in motion to get out of this house, she thought, or else she would lose her mind.

CHAPTER TWELVE

In the early afternoon Beth thought it might be a good time to speak to Sarah about the tenant house. They had been visiting for more than an hour, getting caught up on little tidbits of family gossip. Sarah lounged in the recliner, Beth curled up on the couch.

"This is a lovely house," Beth told her sister. "You did an excellent job decorating."

"It was the therapy I needed after Steven was killed. Thomas suggested that I do it, and I think it may have saved my sanity. He gave me a free hand, and I stretched the project out for months and months." The tight lines on each side of her mouth softened a little. "Poor man. I'm surprised he didn't go stark-raving mad with the house torn up for so long. Thomas is the homebody of the Clary family," she explained. "He'd like nothing better than to marry and have a large family."

"Then why hasn't he?" Beth couldn't hold back the

bite of irritation in her voice. "I doubt he'd have any trouble getting a woman."

"That's true. He's a handsome, virile man, and a beautiful person on the inside."

"Steven was handsome too."

"Yes, Steven had a beautiful exterior." Sarah turned her face away, but not before Beth caught the haunted expression in her eyes.

"I'm sorry I mentioned him. But it's been a couple of years, and I thought—"

"That part of it is all right. I'm not grieving for him. I just have not wanted to talk about that time in my life."

"It's all right. Thomas told me how he was killed."

"Thomas only told you what I asked him to tell you. Now I want you to know it all, and then maybe you'll be more comfortable about Thomas . . . and me."

Beth felt as if the props had been kicked out from under her. "But I'm not . . . I don't . . . you don't have to explain anything to me."

"I want to. I can't help but feel the hostility whenever Thomas's name is mentioned. I want you to stay here, be happy here. The best way to ensure that is to have everything out in the open. The truth is, all the time I was married to Steven, except for the first few weeks, was a living hell. He abused me terribly."

"Sarah!" Beth sat up on the couch, rigid with shocked disbelief. "You don't mean . . . I can't believe . . ." Her voice trailed away as words failed her.

"I'm just now able to talk about it. I know you'll want to know why I stayed with a man who hurt me. Everyone wants to know that. I don't know, now, why I did. At the time I was so humiliated, I couldn't bear the thought of anyone knowing. Deep down inside I felt as if I had failed somehow, or else my husband wouldn't be doing these terrible things to me."

"You could have come home. There was no reason for you to stay here and put up with that!"

"I couldn't! How could I explain to Dad that my handsome, charming husband, who treated me with such loving consideration while in the company of others, had fits of temper and beat me until there were days I couldn't get out of bed?"

"That certainly changes my opinion of the men on this place!" Beth's face was mutinous.

"No one knew about it but Jean, and she didn't find out for a long time. I made her swear not to tell. Jean is a true and loyal friend." Sarah's eyes pleaded with Beth for understanding. "Don't blame anyone but me for what happened here. I could have left him, but I was too big a coward." She paused and swallowed. "Steven was so clever. Usually there were no visible signs of his cruelties. He knew that Thomas would take me away from him if he knew how he was treating me. Thomas was the only person in the world Steven was afraid of."

"I don't know what to say. I never imagined such a thing happening to you. Women have come to the hospital with bruised and swollen faces, broken noses, ribs, arms, legs, and still insisted they loved their husbands and refused to file charges against them." Beth shuddered. "That it could happen to my own sister! How could Thomas *not* have known?" she asked angrily. "Why didn't you tell him?"

"I think Steven would have been furious with me. He always seemed to be competing with Thomas."

"Herb was here. Surely he could see what was going on."

"Herb was having trouble with his wife. She had taken their daughter to Denver and he spent every spare minute down there. Anyway, Steven never allowed me to associate with what he considered the hired help. He disliked Herb immensely and thought him inferior because Herb hasn't had much formal education. He constantly complained that Herb ignored his orders and took orders only from Thomas. The men all liked and respected Thomas, but they didn't like Steven. His explosive temper alienated them. He needed a whipping boy and I was it."

"I've seen the Clary temper in action," Beth said with cold finality.

Sarah smiled. "Thomas's little bursts of temper are nothing compared to Steven's. Thomas is aware he inherited the temper from his father and he never lets it get out of hand."

"I don't know about that." Beth told her about the unnecessary force Thomas had used on the stoned

Jerry Lewis, and about the incident that took place in the cafe during the trip out from Minnesota. "He could have given that boy a concussion."

"But, Beth, dear, he was protecting you. He can't bear to see anyone being mistreated. It riles him quicker than anything." She shifted restlessly, as if her memories were painful. "The night before Steven was killed, he was in an extremely bad mood. That night, instead of beating me on the body and taking his frustrations out on me . . . sexually, he hit me in the face. It was one of the most severe beatings he had ever given me. The next morning I was lying in bed, waiting for Jean to come and help me, when Thomas came to tell me that Steven had been killed on his way to town. I could barely open my eyes to look at him. I remember saying 'I don't care, I don't care.'

"When Thomas saw my condition, and realized what his brother had done to me, he knelt down beside the bed, put his arms around me, and cried." Tears were now rolling down Sarah's cheeks. "Herb and Jean took me to the doctor while Thomas made burial arrangements for his brother. I couldn't attend the services, and I pleaded with Thomas not to notify you. I couldn't bear the thought of you seeing me in that condition. Steven's mother was on a cruise and Thomas delayed notifying her until it was too late for her to come. She had lost a son; there was no need to compound the grief. The doctor, Herb, Jean, and now you, are the only people who know about this.

Thomas and I cling to each other. He's my friend, my brother, and at times, my father." Sarah's face brightened. "I think the world of him."

Sarah went upstairs to rest, and Beth sat on the couch staring into space. She couldn't bear to think of what her sister had been through, the horrible years married to Steven, the silent suffering. She didn't know how Sarah had found the courage to come through such a terrible ordeal. If only she could have helped.

Some of the questions that had nagged her had now been answered. She understood Sarah's feelings for Thomas, and why she'd seldom mentioned her late husband. And she knew the reason behind Thomas's words the night he was sick and she'd held him in her arms. But one question remained. What were Thomas's feelings for Sarah?

"Hey, girls, shake a leg. We're going to have a party!"

Beth heard Thomas's shout despite the fact that her door was closed. She had escaped to her room, having admitted to herself that she was a coward, as soon as she heard Thomas and Herb in the foyer. Now she stood before the mirror, blow-drying her hair, telling herself that understanding the bond between Thomas and her sister would make acceptance easier.

Oh, that's a crock!

A feeling strange to her nature surfaced: jealousy.

Close behind that, guilt all but smothered her. She ground her teeth, despising herself, despising Thomas. There was something special about Sarah. The tragedy of her marriage and her illness would have broken a weaker woman. Sarah deserves all the happiness she can get, Beth told herself sternly.

When Sarah came down the hall to Beth's room looking so beautiful, Beth wished she had worn something else. She tugged the bulky ragknit sweater down over the hips of her jeans and felt gauche and uncomfortable.

"You look lovely. I didn't realize this was a dress-up affair."

"It isn't. But this is a special night for me, and I wanted to dress to fit the occasion." Sarah smoothed her long, maroon velvet skirt, then plucked nervously at the maroon ribbon around the stand-up collar of her frilly white blouse. "Do you think the colors match well enough? Poor Jean hunted all over Cody to find this ribbon."

"It matches your skirt perfectly. But don't you think I should change? I didn't bring a long skirt, but I could wear a dress."

"You're fine just as you are. Oh, Elizabeth, what I wouldn't give to be your age again!" A few seconds later Sarah laughed lightly. "I don't mean that. I wouldn't want to live the last five years over again. This is the happiest time of my life."

And the unhappiest time of mine. Beth kept the thought screened from her face as she kissed her sister's cheek. "Let's go. The Marshall sisters will wow'em tonight."

Beth looked down from the top of the steps and met Thomas's measured look. He stood watching them without a flicker in his eyes to hint at his thoughts. It was the first time she'd seen him since he had left her room early that morning. Butterflies began a boisterous dance in her stomach.

"Careful of the stairs."

"Yes, Father." Sarah's happy laughter rang out.

"Hold onto the railing," he cautioned.

"Thomas and Herb are so afraid I'll fall down these steps that they've forbidden me to come down them unless one of them is here."

"They're right, you know. You shouldn't be using the stairs."

"Hi." The smile on Thomas's face was beautiful. His brilliant green gaze shifted from one sister's face to the other's, then settled on Sarah's. "Welcome home," he said softly, and kissed her cheek. "My, my, don't you look pretty tonight. Did you get all dressed up for me?" His eyes flashed at Beth, and she desperately wished she had worn something more glamorous.

"Sure," Sarah quipped. "I've got to make sure you don't throw me over for my pretty, little sister."

Beth felt the pressure of emotions rising in her throat. Relax, she told herself. Stop being an idiot—Sarah doesn't know.

"I've got a big heart. There's room for both of

you." Thomas moved between them, and with an arm around each, led them into the family room.

Informality was the rule. Beth felt much better about her attire when she saw that every person in the room, including Jean, was wearing jeans and flannel shirts. Flushed and smiling, Sarah greeted everyone and introduced Beth. The names failed to register individually, but collectively they were Jim, Shorty, Frosty, Melvin, and so on, until Beth no longer tried to remember them. Everyone seemed genuinely fond of Sarah and greeted her as if she were returning from a trip around the world. Beth left her with her friends and slipped into the kitchen to offer assistance to Jean.

"Land sakes, no! You're company tonight. I've done 'bout all I'm goin' to. Tom's got the grill goin' in the garage and after a while we'll put on the steaks." Jean's small dark eyes circled the room. "Everybody's here but Herb. He ought to be comin' along."

The ranch hands seemed to be perfectly at home in their boss's house. They milled around, laughing, teasing Sarah about her plants. One of them put a fresh log on the fire, kicked at the grate with his booted foot to shake down the ashes, and replaced the screen. Beth kept her back turned to whichever group Thomas was in, not wanting to meet his eyes, wanting more time to build a barrier against the hurt that was bound to come.

For several minutes she had been aware that

Thomas was stalking her. Finally, when there was nowhere else to go, she stopped circulating and waited. He came up behind her, slipped an arm around her, and rested his hand on her hipbone. Beth lowered her eyes and carefully studied the plates and silver laid out on the countertop.

"How did your day go?" The query was a whisper in her ear.

"Very well. Yours?"

"Busy." A pause. "Are you avoiding me?"

"Hey, Tom, where're the tongs for the salad bowl?" Jean's intervention was a godsend.

Herb came in carrying a large bucket filled with snow and bottles and set it on the counter. Sarah came to greet him, her face radiant. He smiled happily down at her. Beth moved sideways along the counter until she could stand with her back to the wall, watching, but being out of the way.

"Gather 'round, you hungry crowbait." Thomas's voice boomed across the room. "Step up and get a glass. I've an announcement to make."

"Well, I'll be a humpbacked maverick! The boss has bought us champagne!" Charlie, the bowlegged cowboy, led the way to the bar.

Queasiness knotted in Beth's stomach. She stood straight and still while the iron taste of fear rose in her mouth. Fear of what? She didn't have time to answer herself.

The cork flew from the bottle.

Jean jumped and squealed.

The men laughed.

Everyone started to talk at once.

"Step up and get a glass." Thomas spoke to the group in general, but his eyes were on Beth.

She moved into the circle. Someone handed her a glass and reached for another. Beth smiled, feeling like a comet on a collision course.

Thomas held up his glass and waited until the room was quiet. Beth couldn't see his face because he had turned to her sister. Sarah's face was glowing as she looked at him.

"First, I want to say welcome home, Queeny. This ranch isn't the same place without you, love." He kissed her solemnly on the forehead. "Now for the big news." He paused at just the right time and glanced around to make sure he had everyone's attention. His eyes rested briefly on Beth and a handsome, brilliant smile covered his face. Her heart jerked painfully.

"It is with very great pleasure that I announce the engagement and approaching marriage of my lovely sister-in-law, Sarah Clary, to Mr. Herb Rogers. Drink to their future together."

A full ten seconds of quiet followed the announcement. During that time Beth wasn't conscious of taking a breath. She stared at her sister, whose face was lifted for her fiancé's kiss. Her beautiful blond head was nestled against his shoulder, his arms closed protectively around her. Beth couldn't remember ever seeing anyone more radiantly happy.

With tears blurring her vision, she moved forward and embraced both of them. "I'm so happy for you."

"Thank you, darling."

"Why didn't you tell me?" Beth was trying not to cry. She kissed Sarah's cheek, then Herb's. "Welcome to the family. There are three of us now."

"I've loved Herb for a long time," Sarah said, darting loving looks at the tall dark man. "I wouldn't marry him though, until Dr. Morrison assured me my disease was in remission. Thank God, it is!"

"When is the wedding?"

"Soon. Very soon," Herb said emphatically.

Someone came up to pound Herb on the back and offer his congratulations. It gave Beth the excuse to move away. She desperately needed to be alone to blot her eyes and wipe her nose. She walked quickly into the dimly lit living room and stood at the bay window. The yardlight lit the snow-covered land-scape, but all she could see was a teary girl reflected in the window.

Beth's mind was having difficulty grasping and holding on to all that had occurred. *Sarah and Herb!* It could so easily have been Sarah and Thomas. Tears spurted anew. Thomas seemed genuinely pleased that Sarah was going to marry his foreman. Were his feelings being carefully covered, as hers would have been if he'd been the one who was going to marry Sarah? She dabbed at her eyes again, knowing that she should join the celebration going on in the kitchen.

"What's the matter? Why the tears?" Thomas was behind her. He pulled her back against him and pressed his cheek to her wet one. "Aren't you happy for Sarah?" His voice was dear and raspy, and she cried harder.

"Of course I'm happy for her," she said between sniffs. "I wish someone had told me."

"They didn't decide until last night. Herb said they talked for hours on the phone after the doctor told Sarah there was no reason why she couldn't live a reasonably normal life, and maybe in time they'll have a cure for MS. Herb is the best man I know, honey. I wouldn't want anything but the best for your sister." Beth was so choked with feeling that she couldn't talk. "Herb's walking ten feet off the ground," Thomas told her with a chuckle. "He's going to remodel the house down there, make it larger, and have everything on one floor to make it easier for Sarah. She owns a third of the ranch, you know, but Herb isn't one of those men whose pride would keep him from the woman he loves."

"Don't you love her too?" It had to be said. Beth couldn't bear the uncertainty any longer.

"Of course I do. I love her very much. She's the sister I always wanted." He turned her in his arms and lifted her face to his with a firm finger beneath her chin. "Don't tell me you thought I was in love with Sarah."

"You talked about her in your sleep the night you were sick. Naturally I thought that you—"

"What did I say?"

"You said you'd take care of her. That no one needed to know. . . ."

"What else?"

"That's about all. I know, now, why you said it. Sarah told me, but . . ."

"Say it, Elizabeth. I'm tired of you jumping to conclusions and making my life miserable." He gripped her arms and held her away from him so he could stare down into her face.

"I didn't know . . . I don't know where I stand with you!" she blurted.

"Is that the reason for the on-and-off treatment you've been giving me? You thought I was in love with your sister and yet I'd make love to you? I could shake you! Dammit, what kind of a man do you think I am? You put me through hell!" He gave her a couple of shakes and pulled her into his arms. His angry face loomed above hers. He lifted her arms and placed first one and then the other around his neck. "Tell me that you love me, Elizabeth." His eyes met hers and held them steadily. "You love me, so say so, dammit!"

"You big, jerk! Do you think I'd go to bed with you if I didn't?" She watched his face. The frown fell away, and his eyes began to sparkle as smile lines fanned from the corners.

"You ornery little mule! You stubborn, cantankerous, little jackass! Say it!"

"No! Not till you do."

"So help me God, Beth, I'll turn you over my knee. Say it!" He moved his hands down to her hips, his fingers digging into her soft flesh, and jerked her against him so tightly that she could feel the movement of his arousal between them. He turned the full impact of a coaxing smile on her, and she gave in.

"I love you, you . . . peabrain! If you had half the sense you were born with, you'd have seen that I've been eating my heart out for you since the day I drove out of Rochester with you. Stop laughing!"

"Kiss me, Beth."

"And before that, when you came to the wedding—"

"You were just a baby. I was waiting for you to grow up—"

"I was nineteen. You broke my heart!"

"I liked you a lot, but I wasn't ready to settle down. I had to be careful of you because of Sarah. But when I saw you again, it was like I'd been kicked in the stomach by a mule. I tried to tell you, when I sang to you, that day in the truck."

"Will you sing to me again?"

"I don't know. You've put me through the wringer these last few days. Kiss me and stop talking so much—"

"You deserved it—" His kisses swept her words away.

"I love you, darlin'. I thought you knew that. I told you plenty of times," he whispered in her ear, flicking his tongue around the rim. "I'll take care of you always. I'll never hurt you, darlin'." He turned his head to look into her star-bright eyes.

"You don't have to tell me that," she said breathlessly.

"I want to tell you. You never have to worry that . . . I'm like Steven." He held her, eagerly exploring her mouth, before easing her back a few inches so he could see her face.

"I know. I love you."

"I love you." His hands tightened on her hips. "But you're dangerous. How can I go back in there in this condition and tell that bunch there's going to be another wedding?" He cocked one eyebrow in mocking inquiry.

Beth ran nimble fingers over the evidence of his discomfort. "Did I cause *that?*" she wailed.

"Stop that! I'll never be in shape to go back to our guests." It was his turn to wail, but his mouth widened in a slow, satisfied smile.

"Let's not tell them yet," she whispered impishly. "We don't want to steal the spotlight from Sarah and Herb. We'll have our party later."

"Are you propositioning me?" Laughter gleamed in his eyes.

"You bet!"

"Your room or mine?" He kissed her thoroughly and slipped his hand beneath her sweater, searching for her breast with long warm fingers. "I want you to get rid of this thing." His fingers plucked at her bra.

"Now, stop that! Get your sneaky fingers out of there. Someone may come in." Beth's indignant protest turned into a groan of pleasure, then faded into nothingness when she tilted her head to look at his face. It was all there—all the love she had dreamed about. "I wish we didn't have to go back to the party—"

"Beautiful idiot! You're no help at all."